SAFE HARBORS

SAFE HARBORS

Renée Roth-Hano

FOUR WINDS PRESS   NEW YORK
MAXWELL MACMILLAN CANADA   TORONTO
MAXWELL MACMILLAN INTERNATIONAL
NEW YORK   OXFORD   SINGAPORE   SYDNEY

Acknowledgments

I would like to give special thanks first and foremost to the only faithful member left of our writing group—and also my friend—Pascale Retourné-Raab. Her unflinching support and unbiased perspective helped me to maintain the focus on this sometimes painful but always emotionally rich memoir.

I am also deeply indebted to my first editor, Cindy Kane, whose faith and determination helped this sequel to come about, and to Virginia Duncan, Katherine Kirkpatrick, and Jean Karl; their sensitivity and keen vision helped both to enrich and to balance the contents of the manuscript.

I will always be grateful to Sharon Morrison and Jane Hoppen for their continued interest and support and to all those who, knowingly or not, have reached out to me and helped me along the way.

Last but not least, I would like to give special thanks to my husband, John, whose patient and warm support has seen me through trying and joyful times.

Library of Congress Cataloging-in-Publication Data Roth-Hano, Renée, date.
Safe harbors / Renée Roth-Hano.—1st ed. p.   cm. Sequel to: Touch wood.
Summary: Having survived the Nazi occupation of France, teenaged Renée goes to live and work in New York and, while there, begins to come to terms with her Jewish identity and her war experiences. ISBN 0-02-777795-2 1. Roth-Hano, Renée, date.—Juvenile fiction. [1. Roth-Hano, Renée, date.—Fiction. 2. Jews—Fiction. 3. Self-perception—Fiction. 4. New York (N.Y.)—Fiction.] I. Title.
PZ7.R72785Saf   1993 [Fic]—dc20   93-10782

To my sisters Denise and Liliane
To the memory of my mother and father
To the spirit of America

I

WINTER

WINTER 1951

Monday, January 15

I rest my suitcase near the gangplank, the neutral territory between *Liberté*, the ship I am about to leave, and the new land I'm going to tread on. Suzanne and Michael, the two French-speaking strangers who became my inseparable companions on my journey across the Atlantic and made it more bearable, have already been claimed by their families.

I am alone. The cheerful calling, the waving hands from the crowd on the pier below, are not for me. This is a country of strangers—people, for sure, who laugh and cry just like those back home, but strangers just the same. I have had to leave home before, but my sisters were with me then. I feel totally lost in this sea of people who look right past me and who utter words I can't understand. They speak with strange, nasal sounds, not at all like the English I studied in school for more than five years.

The only glimpse I have had so far of New York came earlier today, as our ship entered the harbor: greeting us first, the Statue of Liberty, all by herself in the middle of the icy water, tall and strong and so confident! And then a cluster of majestic, geometric buildings practically sitting on the water. They were breathtaking—but, oh! so cold and impassive!

I've become aware of the icy wind this late morning in January and I raise the collar of my coat. I'm glad I don't have to pretend to be my cheerful self, as Maman always urges me to, or have to agree with everybody how extraordinarily lucky I am to come to America as a governess. "You should be thanking your lucky stars every day for Mrs. Miller's unexpected visit that Sunday afternoon in Paris three years ago," Maman likes to say.

Mrs. Miller had come to our apartment on a Sunday in October to bring us greetings from Molly Singer, a distant relative she'd met while doing volunteer work for a Jewish refugee organization. She visited several times afterward and took such a shine to me that she managed to convince Maman to send me all the way to New York to take care of her ten-year-old daughter, Rita. I am to teach Rita French, and, in turn, Mrs. Miller will sponsor me— that is, guarantee that I won't be a burden to the United States government. This way, I will be able to master the English language properly and get a better job in Paris.

Mrs. Miller also has a twenty-two-year-old son, Murray, an aspiring electrical engineer. "He's the talk of the neighborhood!'' she boasts. She always carries a snapshot of him. I hope she realizes that I am not interested.

One of the stewards of the *Liberté*, who fussed over me during the crossing, dashes past me, waving a hurried *au revoir*—good-bye. It reminds me that I will soon be leaving this floating corner of France to leap into an awesome, dark unknown that may alter my future forever. I suddenly want the world to stand still, time to be suspended—as it was for the five days aboard ship.

The cold, cramped fifth-floor walk-up apartment I shared with my mother and my two younger sisters, even our struggles in postwar Paris, seem paradise to me now. I certainly don't feel cut out to be what everyone expects of me: a sensible, nineteen-year-old girl who is going abroad to perfect her English.

But it is impossible to counter Maman's ideas or decisions. "You need two years—no less—to learn a language," she resolved. I could return home afterward—if that was still what I wanted.

I, for one, thought that one year abroad would be ample. So did my sister, Denise. I can still see her tear-drenched face in the gray, drizzling morning at St. Lazare station, where I was to catch the boat train to le Havre. Lily didn't cry—she never does—but I knew she would be in bed with a stomachache afterward.

No one accompanied me to the boat. We couldn't afford it. It was just as well.

Maman, I know, was eager to send me off. There's no sense fooling myself. There are at least two reasons behind the official one: First, she wants to make sure that I return to the fold. Denise, Lily, and I went into hiding during the war: We stayed with a group of nuns in Normandy. We had to convert to Catholicism to conceal

5

the fact that we were Jewish, and though we pretended to Maman that it meant nothing, after five years we'd still sneak off to church in Paris. Mrs. Miller—Adele—has told us often that America has always welcomed the oppressed, and that New York, in particular, is a wonderful place for Jews.

I hope it will welcome even a confused Jew like myself.

The second reason is that Maman wants to get me away from Fernand. This wonderful boy, young man, brother, friend—all wrapped in one—has been the reason why I get up in the morning and why I sing again. He's managed to bring me out of the shell where I've been hiding since the end of the war, and especially since Papa's death.

Maman is not at all thrilled about Fernand. "He's too young," she says. "And he doesn't have a real profession."

What does she expect at nineteen? He works as a salesman in a fabric store. He's got to make a living! It's tragic enough that his mother, father, and sister died in a concentration camp and that he had to be raised by his Aunt Ida and Uncle Max. Fernand hopes to be a cutter—or better yet, a clothing designer. At any rate, I'm sure that Papa would approve of Fernand, since he himself was a tailor!

Maman and I were at war. She objected every time I was to meet Fernand and *insisted* that I check with her before accepting a date. "We may need you at home!" she'd say.

Imagine! Even my sisters began begging me to stay away from Fernand—if only for the sake of peace.

This is the reason *I* agreed to come to America—to get

away from it all. I will perfect my English while Fernand is studying in a fashion school.

So here I am.

———

The crowd has dwindled down. A uniformed man is motioning. I'm not sure if it is me he is signaling to move forward. A few sounds are coming out of his mouth, twisting it to the side. I can't make out a single word: They all run into one another. I panic, shivering in my coat. How am I going to explain that someone is supposed to pick me up?

I search desperately for the familiar face of Mrs. Miller —she insists on my calling her Adele. She promised to be here. She would even try to bring along her daughter, Rita, she wrote. I am trying to fight the panic. What if she doesn't come? There was that one time when she wrote she would be in Paris by a certain date. I checked daily, in person, at her usual hotel when we didn't hear from her. I even watched every evening through the bedroom window in case a cab would drop her off at our door—only to find out weeks later that she couldn't make it, sorry.

I search desperately through the tears that are now clouding my eyes. My fingers are stiff and cold even with my gloves on. I know the cold comes from inside.

I know very little about America. "It's a place where you can become a success overnight!" a friend of mine, whose uncle settled here, had assured me years ago.

I can't quite figure out how this is possible. I know only what I have seen in the movies: wide-open spaces where wild animals run freely and frontier towns where all the bad guys—and sometimes the good ones, too—get killed in two minutes flat. Of course, there are also Charlie Chaplin's movies, portraying poor people—immigrants—working nonstop and being pushed around.

I prefer Mrs. Miller's—Adele's—view: "It's a golden land where no one goes hungry and where opportunities are open to all."

There's a stir on the pier. My heart leaps with hope. Someone is making her way against the stream of people walking from the ship. She is gesturing wildly and shouting words I cannot understand. It *is* Mrs. Miller—Adele. I recognize her black Persian-lamb coat. How I need her! She is my only link to this new continent. I fly down the gangplank, hardly feeling the weight of the suitcase. She has stopped by the customs officer and shows him some paper. He nods and turns around, signaling me to come forward.

I take the last step. I am hugged and wrapped in Adele's familiar fragrance. I am laughing and crying as I say, "I'm so glad you are here!"—my first English words spoken in New York. She takes my suitcase and explains—in the usual blend of German, English, and French she reserves for me—that there was trouble with the car at the last minute, so she rushed to the pier in a cab.

My cheeks, my fingers are tingling with life again in spite of the icy wind that seeps through every opening. I am ready to brave this new world!

We rush through what looks like a hangar. We are in the street, facing a row of rundown buildings—warehouses, it seems to me. There's an elevated construction over our heads running along the street—a train much like the métro in Paris—that blocks the sky from our view. Fast-moving cars are rushing past.

Adele hails a cab, and soon I sink into the seat. It is comfortable and warm. I wish I could stay nestled like this forever. Outside, the sun is bright, yet the buildings we pass seem dull and lifeless, like boxes with flat tops. No curves, no sloping walls, no shutters at the windows. Some of the buildings have staircases oddly sticking out, with dangling ladders. They make it safer to flee in case of fire, Adele explains. Is fire such a hazard here? I can't help wondering.

We cross larger streets—avenues—numbered in orderly fashion: Tenth, Ninth, Eighth. The people are bundled up in heavy coats and scarves. No dawdling. They rush to wherever they are going.

We are now riding along a park—Tompkins Square Park. The Millers live on the south side, I am told. The taxi stops in front of a light bluish gray apartment building, more cheerful and of more recent construction than any we've passed so far.

We enter the building. The entrance door, which opens with a key, is made of a thick glass pane. The floor is tiled. It is an eight-story building, as I can see from the panel listing the tenants' names. In Paris, the concierge must memorize the names, staircases, and apartment numbers.

I skim over some of the names: Friedman, Cohen. It is funny, I tell myself. I don't like being a Jew, but here I am, looking for a Jewish presence, all the way in New York!

========

There's no one at home. Rita, Adele tells me, is in school and doesn't get back before three-thirty. Good. It will give me a chance to get acquainted with my new surroundings.

9

How warm and cozy the apartment feels after the bitter cold outside. I never got used to the harsh winters of the war years—or the years since for that matter, when coal is still hard to come by—and I always dash for a warm spot like a lizard for the sun.

I step with delight on the thick carpet. Adele takes my coat and scarf and opens a door in the entrance hall: It is a closet *just* for coats! She then leads me into a spacious room where I immediately spot a piano between the two windows—a wonderful surprise. There's also a low glass table between a sofa and a pair of overstuffed armchairs and, against a wall, a console for the television and the radio. A glass door opens out onto an adjoining dining area.

I have never seen such spacious living quarters anywhere, except in the movies. I can't help thinking of our living room-dining room, where the family ate and lived, with just enough space for a round table, six chairs, the enamel stove, and a chest of drawers. It was the only heated room during the long winter months. In the last few years, a piano, rented for my benefit and Denise's, crowded it a little more.

We walk into the kitchen. What a difference from our own windowless, pocket-size kitchen. This one is all bright and sunny; a cheerful yellow curtain drapes the window. There are miles of cabinets and assorted pans pegged onto the wall. Maman and my sisters would not believe it!

Adele has prepared a snack, as she calls it: assorted cold cuts and some yellow cheese, presliced and wrapped individually in cellophane. There's also some sort of shredded cabbage in a sweet dressing, which tastes surprisingly good. Adele watches for my reaction.

"I like it!" I exclaim.

"It's called cole slaw," she informs me.

I don't care for the mushy white bread—all pulp and no crust—but I am hungry. And what am I complaining about, anyway? During the war bread was rationed, and for months after the liberation we had to make do with corn bread, a yellow stuff that got hard as a rock if you didn't eat it immediately.

Besides, this is my first meal here, and I am grateful that I have someone to share it with.

Afterward, I walk over to the piano in the living room. I have been taking piano lessons for four years now—not counting the year of mourning after Papa died—and playing has become my favorite pastime. I hit a few notes— the first chords of "Autumn Leaves." The piano has a lovely sound. Then I turn to Adele, wondering what comes next.

"I'm sorry you won't be able to have your own room just yet," she apologizes. "Murray will be sleeping over for a few days, before joining the military. I'm afraid you'll have to sleep on the living-room sofa in the meantime."

I am positively crushed. How can I be expected to sleep in a public area, so to speak, not only among strangers, but with two men around?

Someone unlocks the entrance door. It is Rita. She throws her schoolbag to the floor, greets her mother with a casual "Hi, Mom!" and walks over to me.

"Hello, Rita!" I say, extending my hand politely, as I would back home.

I don't think she sees my hand. She just looks intently at me, then exclaims, "You must be Renée!" and throws her arms around me in a warm hug that goes straight to my heart.

She is rather pretty, with large blue almond-shaped eyes and a winning smile. She is also a bit chubby. That makes two of us! Adele is quick to point out that the ballet class Rita is taking should help her trim down.

Rita answers with a shrug and follows her mother to the kitchen for a "bite." I sit down next to her.

As she is eating, Rita playfully tests her limited French on me. She names each piece of flatware on the table: *cuiller, fourchette, couteau, verre*—spoon, fork, knife, glass. I am very aware of her looking at me intently as I try to make myself understood in my halting English.

I have the comforting feeling that while we can't converse as yet, we will get along.

"I've learned a lot from Aunt Giza—my mother's sister," Rita confides. "She lived in France before moving to the States."

How odd! I think to myself. Why didn't Adele ever mention her to me?

———

This will be my first dinner *en famille*—with the family.

It's fun giving Adele a hand, getting the soup and the beef stew from the refrigerator—left over from yesterday—and warming them up. I've learned to love leftovers since the war: The food tastes so much better the next day!

What a miracle, this refrigerator, with its many shelves and bins and its freezer, compared to the "refrigerator" at home: the windowsill of the room I shared with Lily and Denise, always cool because it never saw the sun.

"Murray won't be coming home after all," Adele announces. "He called. He's decided to stay with friends. But I'm afraid you'll still have to make do with the sofa, as Murray's things are strewn all over his room!"

It's one less man in the house while I'm quartered in the living room! I think to myself.

As soon as Mr. Miller comes home—he manages a showroom in the garment district—Adele invites us to sit around the kitchen table, which is set with attractive yellow place mats. "Let me greet our Parisian first!" he protests.

He is as I remember him from when I met him briefly in Paris last year: short and stocky, with a head of thick, graying hair, a stern expression on his face. "Welcome to America!" he says, planting a kiss on my cheek. "I hope you'll like it here," he adds. "We'll certainly do everything we can to make it pleasant!"

It is a very nice thing to say.

"Thank you!" I reply.

Mr. Miller then grows silent. He is slurping down his soup, concentrating on the plate before him, as if eager to get it over with. Most of the exchanges are taking place between mother and daughter. It hurts me to see how Mr. Miller and Rita ignore each other.

Ever since my father died, I've become painfully sensitive to seeing fathers and daughters. Whenever I see a father adjusting his daughter's scarf, or a toddler clinging to her father's hand to cross the street, my stomach turns into a knot and a feeling of pain and longing settles into me—and an edge of anger, too, at the unfairness of not having a father.

Adele's voice jolts me back to the present. "I don't like what's been happening with Murray," she remarks. Her tone of voice takes on an annoyed edge as she mentions a certain Evelyn. My ears perk up. Perhaps Murray has a girlfriend?

All Mr. Miller has to say is, "So what?"

She then turns to me. "It's too bad!" she says. "Murray has decided to remain with his friends. I so wanted you to meet him. I know you'll like him!"

Murray is the apple of her eye. There's no doubt about it. But why should she be so concerned about my meeting him—and liking him? She *knows* I'm already spoken for.

His absence suits me just fine. All I want now is his room, a corner I can call my own. The sooner, the better!

I'm lying on the living-room sofa. It is very comfortable, and big enough for two. I'm exhausted, but I can't fall asleep. I'm in strange surroundings in a strange bed. Plush furnishings, thick carpets, a sunny and spacious kitchen, and a cheerful bathroom with pink toilet paper are not enough. I miss home.

How odd that the people who matter most to me are now leading a life that excludes me, while I am experiencing a new world that I cannot share with them. Yet, I decide, remembering Maman's urging to always count my blessings, it *is* extraordinary to be in America. If only she had been less eager to send me off!

I throw a kiss to Fernand's picture, which I sneaked between the metronome and the alabaster statue on the piano. I wonder how I'm going to stand being away from him for so long, when at home I counted the hours from one date to the next?

I tear my thoughts away from Fernand to realize that this is the first time I have had a bed to myself since my return from Normandy, since I used to share a bed with Denise in Paris. Just like that memorable first evening at the nuns', I hug my pillow as if it were a companion and bury my face in it.

"Good-night!" I whisper to myself. "Welcome to America!"

Wednesday, January 17

I am anxious to wake up before anyone else. At least I can use Murray's room to get dressed in. I do my best to be helpful around the house, and I get the coffee under way as Adele, Mr. Miller, and Rita take turns in the bathroom. I want to earn my keep and I certainly intend to pay them back for my cross-Atlantic fare.

I love the toaster: It turns that awful mushy bread into fairly acceptable *tartines*—buttered slices of bread—particularly when I drown them in marmalade.

"But that's *burning* the bread, not *toasting* it!" the Millers tease.

True. But that's the way I like it. It's the closest thing to the *biscottes* back home.

I dash to the bathroom as soon as it is free. I feel positively spoiled to have running hot water and to be able to choose between a shower and a bath—or to take both if I want to. (In Paris, we had to warm up the water we used to wash up daily in the kitchen sink—in the absence of a bathroom—and we had to make do with a weekly visit to the municipal baths.) Especially now that it is so cold outside, I splash with delight under the water for long, wonderful moments.

——————

I don't have to take Rita to school. I just prepare a lunch bag for her—a ham-and-cheese sandwich and an apple. She throws it into her schoolbag, which she slides over her shoulders, and off she rushes to meet her friend right outside the building.

I decide to see Rita off today and to take her down to the door. "Great!" she exclaims. "You'll meet Sally. She's my best friend."

Sally is already waiting by the entrance door—a petite, dark-haired girl with big eyes and long lashes. How pretty she is.

"This is Renée—from Paris!" Rita says.

"Hello," Sally says, flashing a wide smile.

"She'll stop by after school," Rita promises. "Got to go! It's getting late!"

As I watch them walk away, I see myself, too, walking to school with my best friend, Pépée. She lived on the same block and would call out to me from our courtyard. I so looked forward to our walk, with no one breathing down our necks. I was never late.

Images are now racing through my mind, and I am again in Paris, thirteen years old, on the first day of school in October 1944, after an absence of two years. As in the past, Pépée has picked me up. I know I am going to be among my former classmates, and I look forward to seeing my old teachers.

"Those darn boches"—Germans—*"are finally gone, and you'll never have to be afraid again!" Pépée rejoices. "Let's hurry! You don't want to be late on the first day of the* rentrée!"—*the first day of school after the long summer recess.*

Dear Pépée! She is incredible! She never said a word about not hearing from me for two whole years. Of course, she had known from our concierge that my sisters and I fled in the middle of the night to go into hiding and couldn't let anyone know where we were. When I returned, she resumed our friendship as if I had left the day before. We are catching up every day on what happened during all that time.

We are a bit out of breath when we get to school. The front of the building is the same, but the yard is smaller than I remembered it. I recognize Ginette Neveu—her hair is quite long now—and Thérèse Delaunay. She must have grown by a whole head! They both run toward me and kiss me.

"Renée! How have you been? You've grown quite a bit!" Ginette exclaims.

"Where have you been all this time?" Thérèse questions.

"In Normandy," is all I volunteer.

"Oh, really? I have a cousin in Normandy. In le Havre," Ginette remarks. "It's been bombed so many times, there's little left of the old city! Want to join us for hopscotch?" she adds.

"Not right now, thanks!" I reply.

It feels strange, being in the very yard where, two years back, Odile Muller, another schoolmate, eyeing the Star of David I was forced to wear, boasted, "I could have you arrested if I wanted to! My father knows some very important people!"

I was so scared of her after that that I didn't dare refuse to play hopscotch with her whenever she asked me, which was often enough because no one else wanted to play with her. Thank goodness, she is nowhere in sight today.

Then I see good old Mlle Serin, our headmistress, rushing toward me—in her same spike heels, tight curls, and rouged cheeks. "Bonjour, ma petite Renée!" she exclaims, kissing me. "What a young lady you are now. I can't tell you how happy I am to see you! You don't know how often I wondered what happened to you!"

And then she adds, lowering her voice a bit, "Poor little Feigie was not as lucky as you. You probably heard that she was arrested with her parents in that famous roundup in July of *forty-two. She hasn't come back, as far as I know, or she would be here today. How tragic!"*

I don't have time to reply. The bell interrupts us all. Classes are about to begin.

Just as in the old days, I line up next to Pépée, and two by two we enter the building.

Everyone pours into the classroom, settling down noisily in their usual seats. I hesitate at the door. The room is familiar, with its worn wooden desks and spotted inkwells, the unmarked map of France hanging on the wall next to the blackboard. Pépée is saving my seat next to her in the first row and signals me to sit down.

Am I the only one among my classmates to remember Feigie, to see her in her usual seat in the back row, her arms crossed, staring at the open book in front of her? The war may be over for me. But not my struggle to return to normal life.

I suddenly shiver. No wonder! My coat is merely thrown over my shoulders, and I'm still in my slippers!

I rush into the building and up to the warm apartment.

After Rita is gone, Adele sends me to run small errands, as a way to get to know the neighborhood and practice my English. I am very shy about it, but, as Adele points out, it's the only way to learn.

Just as when I first learned stenography and playfully transcribed every word into the coded signs, I am deciphering every English word, sign, or inscription that comes to my attention.

There's nothing exciting about the neighborhood. Take Avenue A, for instance, where most of the stores are. They must have run out of ideas when they named the avenues in alphabetical order. By comparison, the streets of Paris have such interesting names—like rue des Lavandières, "street of the washerwomen"; or rue de l'Arbre-Sec, "street of the dried-out tree." They have stories to tell, and they talk to us about the past.

The past also lives in all the buildings, the churches, the squares. From our Paris neighborhood, we can walk to the *Grands Boulevards* or to Pigalle. We live minutes from the famous Sacré-Cœur basilica, built on a hill and overlooking the whole of Paris. My favorite promenade consists of a grand tour of nearby Montmartre on a Sunday afternoon: We climb up the many steps to Sacré-Cœur, stopping at each terrace to embrace Paris at our feet. Then we go around the *butte* Montmartre and spot on the way the streets and corners immortalized by the world-famous painters Utrillo and Toulouse-Lautrec, proud to have all this at our fingertips.

In contrast, the candy store on Avenue A where I get the *Daily Mirror* is a shambles of newspapers piled up on the floor, of candies and chewing gums lined up on the counter, of shelves crowded with canned food and bottles—all very dull and boring. It certainly doesn't invite any lingering or exploring. Nor do the shopkeepers, for that matter. No one asks the customers about their last born, their dogs, or the state of their colds; you just pick up what you want, pay for it, and leave.

The grocery store where I pick up the milk is a bit more interesting. I spotted a box of matzohs—in January, in full view of everyone—casually set between the rice and the flour! In Paris, you can only find matzohs during Passover week—and then only in a specialized store, in the Pletzl, the small Jewish neighborhood where mostly pious Jews live.

Eating matzohs during Passover is the only Jewish tradition we have observed at home since the end of the war. As far as I can tell, the Millers are not any more observant. The only sign of Jewishness I've noticed so far is the mezuzah on their door.

No matter how far I walk, all the shops look exactly the same to me—the cleaners, the grocery stores, the candy stores, the delicatessen; all carrying the same stands, the same display units, the same counters— down to the identical neon signs reading LIQUORS, BREYERS ICE CREAM, DELI. They have no charm whatsoever. Neither do the straight, uniform streets, without curves, bends, or slopes. If there were no nameplates to distinguish one from the other, I'd surely get lost!

One good thing here: You can buy fruit in ones or twos, and even pick out your own. In France, you wouldn't dare buy in any way but by the pound or the kilo. My sister Denise would just love buying fruit here. She hates any fruit that is too ripe or is spotted.

Monday, January 22

I am all excited. For the first time in the week I've been here, I have been able to understand what the radio announcer was saying: "No money down! . . . No money down! . . . Six months to pay!"

Mr. Miller—he insists on my calling him Stanley, but it doesn't come easy—roared when he heard me exclaim about it.

"They're pushing the idea of buying on credit," he

20

said. "Funny that you should pick *that* up! It certainly says something about the times we live in!"

I, for one, wanted to hug the radio.

=========

It takes me by surprise. For a split second, I hear behind me, as I am going down Avenue A, someone speak French. I swing my head around and, before I know it, my eyes well up with tears and all I want is to run to the person, pull his sleeve, and tell him: "Hey, I am French, too!"

What am I doing here? Feeling suddenly out of place in these uniform streets and look-alike shops, and blinded by tears, I run all the way home.

I have received only one letter so far from my family, and none from Fernand. I don't want to hear that the mail gets delayed. I am so angry at Fernand that I have turned his picture to the wall.

More than my red eyes, Adele notices my sullen mood after I have returned.

"What's wrong?" she finally asks.

"I miss home!" I sniffle, concentrating on the tomatoes and radishes I'm slicing for tonight's salad.

"What's there to miss?" Adele snaps. "So it takes a while to get used to New York. Just give it some time. Your life in Paris wasn't *that* rosy, as far as I could tell!"

Of course, it *wasn't* that rosy, but what's that got to do with anything? How do I explain that not everything in France is bad and not everything here is perfect—even if it is easier. I simply miss Paris. Here, I walk, but I have no direction. My eyes and ears search for something familiar, but I don't recognize anyone or anything. I am no one's daughter, no one's sister, no one's loved one. I am nothing.

"That may be so," Mr. Miller counters his wife. "But she is homesick just the same! Look, this is a new country, with different people and customs—and a new language, for God's sake. Have you forgotten?"

I like this man! I think, relieved that someone understands what's happening and doesn't see it as my being ungrateful.

"What Renée needs," he continues, "is to get out of the house, see people, and get to know the rest of New York. Your sister Giza would certainly be good company—and someone she could speak French to."

This is the second time I hear about Adele's sister—oddly enough, not from Adele.

For once, Adele agrees with her husband. She will call her sometime soon. "I don't really get to see Giza that often," she explains. "We don't have too much in common. But I'm sure she'll be thrilled to meet someone from France. She's a few years younger than I am and still lived with my mother in Vienna when I came to the United States. They moved to France, where they lived a few years while waiting for their American visas."

What never fails to amaze me is how so many Jews go from country to country without ever being given a chance to grow roots—uninvited guests who won't leave—only to end up in the States, where they all stay.

Adele then adds cheerfully, "Anyway, Murray is supposed to arrive here late this evening. Finally!" She sighs. "And I know he'll be good company."

Murray does make an appearance late tonight. He certainly doesn't have Fernand's striking good looks, but he has a rather pleasant face. He has Rita's pale-blue almond-shaped eyes and his mother's smile. He is a bit cocky as he parades around in his impeccable khaki uniform with its shiny buttons.

"I'm so happy to meet you—I've read all your letters to Mom!" he exclaims—but his mother cuts him off angrily—I can tell more from her tone of voice than from the words. The name Evelyn comes up again and again, and it is soon clear that the friend with whom he was staying is a girl. He patiently takes Adele's hand in his and talks to her as if to a child: "Now, Mom. We've gone over this before. Let me handle it my way!"

All this makes me rather uncomfortable. I feel I'm eavesdropping on a private conversation. But no one seems to mind my presence.

Adele continues her tirade, and Murray finally leaves the room in a huff, shouting, "I don't want to hear another word!"

Mr. Miller remains silent until he finally explodes, "Why can't you leave him alone? He's a man now!"

But Adele doesn't give up.

She calls up a bunch of girls—Sandy, Beverly, Diana—inviting them over one by one.

"Murray is home for a couple of days!" she tells them. "Come on over to say hello!"

"They just love him!" Adele confides to me. "Before you came to New York, they used to flock to baby-sit for Rita just to have a chance to see him!"

I'm rather shocked at the whole idea. She used these poor girls to watch over Rita, and now she is using them again to divert Murray from that girl Evelyn, whom he clearly likes.

I'm suddenly seeing Adele in a new light and I don't like it. I hope she won't use *me* that way!

Tuesday, January 23

This evening, after Beverly's visit with Murray, Rita tells me why her mother is so determined to battle her brother: "Evelyn is Catholic—and older than Murray. But she's crazy about him. And she's nice to me, too."

I can't blame Adele for not wanting her son to become serious about a gentile girl. There's no way *I* could ever trust a non-Jew enough to marry him, not after all I've been through.

Maman would certainly like to hear me say that!

But doesn't Adele see that she's going about it the wrong way? All she does with her carrying on is throw Murray right into Evelyn's arms!

Friday, January 26

I know that Murray has been watching me—I caught him looking at me on the sly a few times, and so I'm not surprised when he offers to take me on a ride to Queens, at the whispered suggestion of Adele in the kitchen after dinner. For a moment, I wonder what the two of them are up to, but I have no reason to object to the idea. Murray just wants me to see the view of the New York City skyline that unfolds as one crosses the bridge back over to Manhattan.

"Have a good time!" Adele says, pushing me toward Murray.

The car is parked around the corner—a heavy, light-blue affair with sturdy, reassuring fenders. The cars are so much larger here than in France.

I settle into the seat next to Murray with a mixture of excitement and apprehension. After riding for a few blocks, I relax, eager to discover the town. Murray is a good driver.

We stop for coffee at a diner—typical of New York, Murray explains. Clearly, Murray wants to talk. Before sitting down in one of the booths, he puts a coin into the jukebox. I know it will be country music—something Adele abhors and nags him about.

I let him talk. He's unhappy about going into the military. The draft is compulsory. There's no way he can avoid it. In France, joining the army is compulsory, too, and every young man must enlist the day he turns twenty. But the situation here is more serious—it is much clearer to me now, and I feel truly sorry for Murray: The United States is involved in the Korean "conflict," a war thousands of young men are being sent to fight in. He fears being one of them. Maybe he thinks he'll never come back?

"I guess having to leave Evelyn makes it even harder," I venture. I don't want to pry, but I feel uncomfortable, and I *have* to mention Evelyn's name.

"I see that you've heard about her. God knows, my mother makes enough of a fuss over her!"

Suddenly, his hand is on mine. I withdraw it instantly. What is he up to now?

He doesn't try again, but on the way back, he stops the car on a quiet, tree-lined street. I am getting terribly uncomfortable. All I want is to get home.

He puts his arm around me and, before I know it, he draws my face to his—just like in the movies.

"What are you doing?" I protest, freeing myself from his hold, my heart racing. Is that what he and Adele were concocting in the kitchen? I wonder, feeling positively betrayed by both.

"What's the big deal?" Murray laughs. "I like you—I really do! And I think you like me. I want to get to know you better, that's all! Come on, Renée. It's only a kiss!"

What does he mean, *only* a kiss?

"Well, I'm sorry, but it's a big deal to me!" I counter. To me, kissing—I mean kissing on the lips—is terribly important. It's a decisive step that should evolve naturally in a relationship, just like switching from the formal *vous* to the more intimate *tu* when addressing someone.

Obviously, Murray doesn't appreciate such subtleties. I can't figure out these strange people—Americans—who are so formal and stiff in public places and think nothing of grabbing you the minute there's no one around.

"Besides," I add, recovering my poise, "I have a boyfriend in Paris. You know about him. And what about Evelyn?"

"So what?" Murray persists. "You're not engaged. Neither am I. Come on, we're both adults."

He should only know! I think to myself. He should only know how much patience, cajoling, and reassuring it took from Fernand for me to agree to our first kiss. I was very frightened—and rightly so. God knows, my feelings for Fernand were overwhelming enough for me without complicating them any more.

"We have all the time in the world!" Fernand had said. He always seemed to say the right thing. The words worked like magic. In time, my reserve melted—but only with him.

"I may not be engaged to Fernand, but I certainly feel committed to him!" I announce proudly, trying bravely to meet Murray's stare. "How about going home now?"

I suggest, gathering all I can to make my voice sound strong and firm. The last thing I want is for him to know how shaky I feel inside.

As Murray and I enter the apartment, I sense Adele's questioning eyes. Murray simply says that we stopped for coffee and that I had been so taken by the New York skyline that I wanted to return to Queens so that we could cross the bridge all over again. All of which is true. We leave it at that.

"Are you going to marry Murray?" Rita whispers into my ear later, when I kiss her good-night.

I look at her, stunned by her question. What is this? I think to myself. A conspiracy?

Saturday, January 27

Adele doesn't like me to dawdle. But today, I'm in no hurry to take care of the same chores: Do the breakfast dishes, straighten out the beds, scrub the sink and the bathtub, put Adele's jars in order—day creams to the right, night creams to the left—reorganize the drawers she wrecks daily, go over her shirts to spot the missing buttons. Adele! Always Adele!

And I'm in no hurry to have her watch my every move: "You waste much too much soap on those dishes!" she scolds.

I *do* like to plunge my arms into the sudsy water just for the fun of it. You can tell she didn't really live through the troubles of the war years, when soap, a prized find to begin with, was hopelessly sudsless. So I let her complain.

Adele hates to see me idle and makes sure I don't run

out of things to do. Today, polishing the silver is on the agenda.

I need some time to myself because I can't get Murray's words out of my head. Did I really make a mountain out of a molehill over that silly kiss? He must have known that I meant what I said, though, since he left me alone the rest of the evening.

Rita—who is off from school today—insists on doing errands with me this morning, even though I warned her that I need some time to myself in order to gather my thoughts. What I didn't tell her is that I need to think through my incident with Murray last night.

We stop in front of a redbrick building squeezed between two brownstones. It has two large stained glass windows on either side and a dozen wide steps leading to a large wooden gate. A huge cross sits on the tiled roof.

"Do you mind if I stop here? I'll only be a few minutes," I ask Rita.

"But it's a church!" she exclaims, obviously not knowing what to make of it.

Of course, it is a church. That's precisely why I want to stop here!

"I know it is. It's the first Catholic church I've come across since I've been in New York, and I'm curious to see what it's like," I explain.

"But you don't *have* to go in anymore!" Rita insists, following her own quite understandable logic.

"I know I don't *have* to. I really *want* to," I further explain, wanting her to understand. "I have warm memories of churches in Normandy—going to mass and to vespers on Sundays, chanting and praying and all that."

This is hardly the time to get into such a serious subject—and the last thing I want is to confuse Rita by further explaining that my sisters and I, while we never forgot that we were Jewish, felt accepted by the nuns and in church in a way we never had been before.

"I don't go to the synagogue as often as Candy, but when I go, I feel at home, too," Rita reflects.

"Good for you. You're very lucky," I say. "I wish I'd felt that way as a child, but the war changed all that. Besides," I add spontaneously, "we *did* become Catholic." Do I feel I need to apologize?

"Come on, Rita! We must hurry," I urge, not wanting to pursue the conversation any further. "Just wait here," I say, rushing to climb the steps.

"Wait! Wait!" Rita cries out, holding me back by the hand. "I never knew that you became Catholic!" she exclaims, looking intently at me as if she is seeing me for the first time.

"I don't like to talk about it. Most people don't understand it. You see, when we were hiding in the convent, no one was to find out that we were Jewish, so we prayed and went to church. But that's all. Then, one morning, Mother Superior told us that we would be baptized. The Germans had come to Flers and were parading all over town. The curé baptized us so that we were able to take communion and go to confession, like everybody else. We had to be invisible! What else were we to do?"

"So what are you now?" Rita wants to know. "Catholic or Jewish?"

It *is* a good question, I admit to myself, although no one has ever before asked me about it that bluntly.

Had I been asked the question after our return from the convent, I would most certainly have replied, "Catholic." The three of us insisted on attending Sunday mass in the neighboring Paris church of St. Vincent de Paul—the patron saint of our nuns—first on the sneak, and then openly, against Maman's arguments and Papa's threats.

I wasn't merely running away from the pain of being a Jew, or being a rebellious thirteen-year-old. I was also hurt and disappointed that my parents so readily dismissed our two years of exile—two years during which Denise, Lily, and I felt abandoned by them and barely survived hunger, illnesses, and bombings.

"We'll try to forget about those bad times and pick up our life where we left off!" Papa had declared.

How could we?

"I consider myself a Jew, of course," I finally reply, "but I also have a fondness for churches! Look, we could go on talking forever, but it's getting late," I remind Rita. "Just give me a few minutes and wait for me here."

"No . . . I'm coming with you!" Rita decides.

It is strange that after all these years, I still seek out a church as a safe retreat, even though my faith has long vanished.

Inside the church I shut my eyes to better savor the familiar odor of incense and burned candles that wraps around me.

I'm back in St. Jean's church in Flers. How I love the sight of men, women, and children worshiping together, praying in unison. How I love joining in the hymns, singing at the top of my voice, with all my soul, hoping, in spite of everything, that somehow God will step down and make everything all right again.

And then, on D day, it happens.

After the short-lived excitement of the Allies' landing in the wee hours of the morning, we are gathered in the hallway, crying, praying frantically as the bombs fall all around us. Denise, Lily, and I are clinging to Sister Madeleine, holding hands one last time, waiting to die. Then I do this incredible thing: I promise God that if he lets us live, I will become a nun!

We survive. So, for five long years afterward, I walk around, carrying my secret, begging God to set me free from the vow. I have too many unanswered questions, too many doubts about God himself.

And then, one day, the calling vanishes—as does my belief in God. At first I feel relieved. But then I become lost, confused, with a big void in me and without a clear idea of where I belonged. What am I? A Jew? A Catholic? A little bit of both? Neither?

And then Fernand comes along and gives new meaning to my life.

I open my eyes. From the back of the church, where I'm still standing, I embrace the altar; the statue of the Virgin Mary to the side; the tall, lonely candle in the corner, flickering but never giving up.

I feel much calmer and see things much more clearly now. So I'm *not* as strong and grown-up as they all make me out to be!

Maybe Murray's taking me across the Queensborough Bridge the second time was his way of saying "I'm sorry"? Let him go in peace.

———

I look for Rita, still standing just inside the entrance gate, and motion her to leave.

"Did you pray?" she whispers as we are walking out.

"No. I just thought things through. But it helped," I whisper back.

I take her hand and we dash off.

Monday, January 29

I am becoming obsessed with words. English pronunciation is very tricky. The way you accent the word determines whether you will be understood or not. The trouble is, English words are accented differently from French words.

"Where are the vegetables, please?" I bravely asked the man at the fruit stand yesterday, pronouncing it the only way I knew how, the French way: vege*ta*bles. He looked at me, utterly puzzled. He had no idea what I was talking about. Some bystander kindly bailed me out. "Ah, you mean *veg*etables! They're inside."

I cannot take anything for granted!

I am trying to match the spoken word with the written one whenever I get a chance to listen—in conversations at home, on the radio, in the street. I am also self-conscious about some sounds I know I can't pronounce correctly: the *th*, the *r*, and some of the vowels. They say that the sounds you learn as a very young child are hard to unlearn and that new sounds don't come easily. I guess I'm stuck: I can't distinguish, for the life of me, the difference between *collar* and *color*. Rita says it's easy. But then, *she* can't get the French *u* straight or pronounce the French *r* correctly. We are even!

One blessing in all this: While I am hesitant about finding the right words or getting them in the right sequence in English, I'm not as shy or as emotional as in French. They are just new words, new labels. They're not attached to feelings—yet.

Friday, February 2

Rita is good company. I watch over her like a big sister, making sure she gets her homework done before she's allowed to settle in front of the television with either of her friends, Candy or Sally. I also see to it that she practices her scales and her Czerny finger exercises at the piano—Adele's order—which she hates.

"Do I *have* to? It's so boring!" she complains.

So we struck a deal: When she has worked extra hard at her practicing, we play duets together. She loves it. I do, too. It makes me think of the Diabelli duets Denise and I enjoyed in Paris after dinner. I always played the left hand and she played the right hand.

You can't get Rita to help around the house! I'm always after her to tidy up her room or to pick up the clothing or books strewn about—her only responsibility! The other day I ran around the room to catch her: "All you care about is washing and setting your hair every day, or wearing angora sweaters and socks to match!" I scolded. All Rita did was giggle.

I've noticed girls in the street wear stockings, lipstick, and even mascara. At twelve or thirteen! It makes them look so much older! All I did for my dates with Fernand was apply a pale lipstick. And, when Maman and my sisters were not looking, I squeezed an orange peel straight into my eyes: I read somewhere that it was guaranteed to make them sparkle.

33

Children here are definitely of a different species: I can't get used to their slamming the door in my face. Nor can I get used to Rita's friend Candy helping herself to a soda from the Millers' refrigerator without asking anyone's permission.

They're just spoiled, I tell myself. But, deep down, I envy their arrogant confidence, their quiet expectation, much as I did with my friend Pépée in the past. How I admired her poise as she entered a room full of strangers, or the simple and direct manner in which she addressed the class from the blackboard, or even the assured and energetic way she rolled down avenue Trudaine on her skates or threw her ball far and high, while I merely struggled along.

"You can, too, if you want to!" Pépée had declared.

Not so! I protested silently. This unshakable confidence *has* to come from the inner conviction that tomorrow is something to look forward to, that any difficulty will eventually be worked out, and that no major upheaval is ever going to shatter the world.

=====

The television is fascinating. I never saw one before. It's like having a movie screen in your own living room. But Rita likes to watch cartoons in the late afternoon, and I can't get too excited about those.

My favorite time of the day is the evening, after the dishes are done and everything is put away, when Rita and I retire for an hour or so to her room and speak French.

She has a lovely room—a whole room to herself—with a large closet all her own. Such luxury! There's a big brass bed in the middle, a night table, and, between the windows, a small desk and a bookshelf. On the opposite mirrored wall, there's a metal bar for her stretching exercises. She loves ballet and is forever showing off new steps. Plié. Sauté. She is surprisingly graceful as she arches her arm over her head or stretches her leg back into an impeccable arabesque.

What I like best—but I keep this to myself—is her collection of dolls nestled into the rocking chair by her bed. I favor the dark-haired one, Melanie—so much like Jackie, the only doll I ever owned. We had brought her with us when we fled from Alsace, and I managed to sneak her into my suitcase all the way to Normandy, only to lose her in the bombings of D day.

Rita likes me to read her "Little Red Riding Hood" and "Sleeping Beauty" in French. Her eyes are riveted on me. She rounds up her lips to mimic the sounds and sighs at the critical moments.

"*Chaperon rouge, chaperon rouge,*" she repeats tirelessly, trying to get the *r*'s right.

=====

Tonight, though, as I settle into the rocking chair, I'm in no mood to read to Rita: We've had our first run-in, and I feel upset.

It was after dinner. Adele had retired to her room to make some phone calls. I had cleared the table, done and put away the dishes, tidied up the kitchen. Stanley was sitting in his favorite armchair, absorbed in his newspaper, while Rita was sprawled on the floor, watching TV.

I had just sat down on the sofa when Rita said, "Renée, bring me a glass of water!"

"I just sat down, Rita. And you're closer to the kitchen. Why don't you get your own water?" I snapped.

"That's what you're here for!" she shot back.

"No, it's not! And it would be nice if you could say 'please'!"

How I wished Stanley had backed me up. But he didn't. He was too absorbed in his reading—or he didn't care to get involved. Here, too, I felt let down.

"Please, Renée, please!" Rita implored, having lost the edge in her voice. "I don't want to miss any of the show."

Without a word, I got up, stepped over her, and walked to the kitchen to get her a glass of water.

=====

"Why don't we skip the lesson," I suggest now, getting up and tucking her in. "I'm tired tonight."

"Don't leave me yet," Rita begs, sitting up on her bed. "Are you still mad at me? Please," she insists, throwing her arms around me, "tell me a new story. Tell me about when you were a little girl!"

I hug her, too, grateful for the tender feelings that are rushing back.

"Maybe another time. I *do* feel tired tonight," I apologize.

"I want to know more about you and your sisters. Mummy says that you all had a very rough time."

I wish I could tell her. But what happened during those years is not your average tale to be told before bedtime.

As I look at Rita lying on her bed, her head propped on her elbow, my mind travels back in time, and I see myself lying on a blue polka-dot pillow next to my sister Denise in Mulhouse, watching the small lamp on the light-blue dresser because I was afraid of the dark, finding comfort in Alex (our teddy bear) and our doll, Jackie, nestled in the puffy blue-velvet armchair.

How can I put into a coherent and logical whole the

unexplainable—that I went to bed one night as an ordinary eight-year-old and woke up the next day as a Jew, forced to leave the only home I ever knew?

What did I know then about being Jewish, other than going to the synagogue on Rosh Hashanah and Yom Kippur, the High Holy Days—and then having to sit away from Papa and the men to boot!—or being asked to leave the classroom when Catholic instruction was given, or the firm conviction that Jews seemed to prefer boys to girls?

"Well, won't you tell me?" Rita insists, tugging at my sleeve, bringing me back to the present.

"It's not a happy story, and I'm not sure you'd want to hear it before going to bed."

"Tell me! Tell me! I'll be all right."

I settle back into the rocking chair, pushing the dolls to the side.

"I don't know where to start," I say, "except that my whole world came apart on the day when World War Two broke out—that is, when France declared war on Germany. I remember. It was a nice day in September. We were all sitting around the table in the little bungalow where we spent our summers, having lunch, when there was an announcement on the radio. I was only eight and I had never paid much attention to the radio before, but after that everyone around us acted so strange that I knew that something dreadful was happening." I pause to let out a deep sigh.

"You really remember when the war started?" Rita asks, somewhat in awe. "What happened then?" She is watching me intently.

"Everything. . . . And so fast!" I need to pause again, and let out another sigh.

"You know, from the start, there were air raids almost daily and we were forced to wear gas masks—to go to school, to go everywhere—just in case the Germans were to use gas as a weapon, as happened during World War One. The masks frightened me to death with the hose hanging down the nose: I just couldn't get myself to breathe with the silly thing on! And they weighed a ton! But the real trouble began when France surrendered to the Germans—about nine months later. The Germans were to annex Alsace—the part of eastern France where we lived—and that meant that Jews were in trouble."

"I remember Mummy telling me that's why *she* left her own country, Austria. And that was even before the war!" Rita remarks.

"You're right. The Germans—I should say, the Nazis—began to make trouble for the Jews as early as 1933, which is when Hitler came to power, six years before World War Two started. By the way, Hitler himself was from Austria," I point out. "You *have* heard about Hitler, haven't you?"

"You mean that awful man with the mustache who screamed anti-Jewish slogans at rallies?" Rita offers.

"Right! The point I'm trying to make is that, until then, I didn't feel very different from any other kid. Almost overnight, being Jewish became a nightmare: We were forced to leave town—we had three days to get out and we had our blind grandmother with us. I'll never forget the day we left. A van was taking us away, and I looked with envy at a bunch of girls rushing out of school. Was the war only on for us? I remember thinking. I didn't want to leave and I didn't know whether we'd ever come back."

"I could never leave here!" Rita exclaims, looking around her familiar surroundings. "I couldn't do without my old pillow, my dancing shoes—my everything!"

"I didn't think I could, either," I whisper to myself. "But I'm sure you won't have to!" I quickly add, hoping with all my heart that no other children will ever have to.

"Did you go to Paris then?" Rita questions.

"Yes, we did. We were lucky. My mother had some childhood friends there, and they helped us get settled. Paris was a big city, a place where they left the Jews alone, we had been told. Well, Paris turned out *not* to be safe after all. The Germans had taken over Paris and a good half of France and ruled over it. Anti-Jewish decrees started to pour over us one after another: First, we had to register at the police station; then we couldn't have a radio, travel freely, or be out past a certain hour. In time we were banned from movies, parks, cafés, stores—like a bunch of lepers in danger of contaminating others!"

I know my voice is rising and I am getting upset. I swallow hard.

Rita doesn't say a word. But she doesn't miss anything.

"What *really* got to me," I continue, "is when we were forced to wear the Star of David."

"You mean like this?" Rita questions. She reaches for the drawer in her night table and pulls out a gold chain with a small star on it.

"Yes. Except that it was as big as the pocket on your pajamas and had to be sewn onto our jackets or our coats for everyone to see. Believe me, it wasn't meant for decoration, but to humiliate us. I was so ashamed that I became very quiet and couldn't look people in the eye. I remember how I skimmed the walls, frightened by the stares of people in the street, in school, in the subway. I saw eyes everywhere!"

"How awful! This could *never* happen in America!" Rita exclaims. "Why couldn't you complain to the president of France? I would have written a letter to him! He was still in charge!"

"That was my reaction, too . . . at first, at least. . . . But the French officials at the time were no better than the Germans and were quite willing to go along.

"Actually," I reflect, "I very vividly remember the ugly posters displayed all over town that showed caricatures of Jews—you know, with hook noses, thick lips, crooked nails. And how the newspapers and magazines published daily insulting articles or remarks about Jews. It was all very official."

For a moment, my thoughts drift away. I can't help thinking of my father, who was long convinced that this was all vicious propaganda, the work of a bunch of fanatics.

"What are you thinking about?" Rita questions.

"I was thinking of my father. . . . He was the last one to give up hope. Until that fateful day during July of 1942—it was a Thursday—when, without any prior warning, thousands and thousands of Jews were picked up from their homes early in the morning, driven away in busloads to a huge stadium, and then interned in a camp near Paris—to be shipped later to other camps in Germany and Poland, where they were to be killed. *Labor camps,* they called them at the time. Among these people were dozens of dear friends and neighbors . . . including Monique, the two-year-old daughter of my father's friend, and my little classmate Feigie."

I suddenly find myself reaching for Melanie—Rita's doll—at my side. She *does* remind me of my doll, Jackie, I reflect, squeezing her against my chest—and, with her black hair and chubby legs, a little bit of me.

"I'm sorry," Rita whispers. "What was she like?"

I welcome Rita's questions. They force me to focus on concrete details about Feigie.

"She had a narrow face and a marked cleft in her chin. But she was extremely shy. In class, she'd never say anything unless the teacher asked her and she kept pretty much to herself. It was only when trouble started for the Jews and we found out we both were Jewish that we began to talk. We would go and look at the anti-Jewish graffiti on a building near school or talk about the latest happenings. And then one day she walked up to me and, point-blank, asked me if I wanted to have dinner at her home. I did, of course. Her mother and father were so happy about our friendship, and I remember how she smiled. . . . I never got a chance to see her home again."

Mindlessly, I pat Melanie's hair.

Rita is staring at me, speechless.

"How do you know that she isn't alive today?" she finally whispers.

"I'm sure she isn't. Few people, least of all children, survived the Auschwitz camp—we learned much later that that was where they were all shipped. That's also where my mother's two older brothers died. They were deported there from Hungary. . . . For a whole year after the war, my mother kept hoping daily for mail from them. But then she stopped talking about them. I wish I had known them better," I reflect, feeling unexpected longing for these uncles I never knew and their wives and children. "You know," I add, my voice unsteady by now, "for the longest time, I kept seeing Feigie walking up to me, her books under her arm, like she did the time she invited me for dinner." I'm outright crying by now. "She was only eleven—about your age," I whisper.

"Don't cry, Renée. I might cry, too!" Rita protests, throwing her arms around me.

"I think it's best to stop for now . . . and high time to get to bed!" I declare. "I promise to stay here until you fall asleep."

Who would want to be Jewish after that? I ask myself as I watch Rita getting settled in the dark, confident in the world around her.

Sometimes, like tonight, I would give a lot to be able to get excited about cartoons or angora socks or the right color lipstick—or even about a card game with my sisters back home.

Rita's even, easy puffs signal her being asleep. I lean over her and pull the blanket to her shoulders. I tiptoe out and, as I cast a last glance before leaving the room, I hope that, some day, I will be able to forgive Rita, Candy, and all the children this side of the Atlantic for having the wonderful fortune of growing up in times of peace and enjoying the carefree days of a childhood I could never have.

Monday, February 5

Today, getting the newspaper from the candy store, I saw a young boy walk hurriedly down Avenue A with a yarmulke on his head. In Paris, no one wears one in the street, only in the synagogue. For a fleeting moment, I felt my heart pounding, like in the old days. I wanted to run after him and yell, "Are you crazy, flaunting your Jewishness this way? Don't you know you're asking for trouble?"

What was incredible was that no one paid any attention—no one appeared to even *see* him! I couldn't take my eyes off him until he vanished from sight.

I often wondered, after the war was over, as I came across people in the street in Paris, whether this one or that one *really* saw us as monsters, if the French, like the Germans, had been brainwashed by the newspapers, the vile propaganda? There were, of course, courageous people, like my friend Pépée; our neighbors, the Chavignats; and the nuns who risked their lives by taking us in.

There were many of those—little, humble people. But there were many, too, who informed on Jews, like those horrible neighbors who denounced my uncle and aunt in Moutiers.

Despite the peace, anti-Semitism is still frightening to me: It is a smoldering, senseless hatred at its ugliest.

At least here, in New York, perhaps I can begin to relax. People don't seem to be obsessed with Jews.

I must write home about that!

Monday, February 12

Receiving mail has become the highlight of my days. I am particularly spoiled today: I have a letter from Denise and two from Fernand.

Denise has been writing to me faithfully, always concluding with a little phrase in steno—our secret code—commenting on Maman's mood.

Denise and I happen to like the same things—movies, for instance. But most of all, we just love to dance. We managed to convince Maman to let us take a series of ballroom-dancing classes. We both especially liked the Latin dances. We had fun doing the dip and turning our heads back and forth during a tango, or languidly moving our hips while doing the rhumba. We used to samba or rhumba our way home. One evening, we even danced in the snow!

"I hope we'll never get so old that we won't be able to dance, and that the man I'm going to marry will like to dance, too!" I confided.

"You'll always have me," Denise replied.

In today's letter, my sister tells me about her job—this is her first job, and she loves it. It's a small business and, efficient and well-organized as she is, she has been given a lot of responsibility. However, the heating situation continues to be a problem, she tells me. In the absence of coal, her boss is using petroleum to heat the office. The fumes are so unbearable, though, that they must keep the windows open for ventilation. They're all keeping their coats and gloves on so as not to freeze!

Lily, she further writes, is enjoying her last year at a high-fashion trade school and should be able to land a fine job when she graduates.

I think about Lily. It wasn't easy growing up with a sister—the youngest, yet!—who is everything I want to be: thin as a rail, cool and collected, even in her run-ins with Maman, and accomplished in just about everything she touches. Her key *never* gets stuck in the keyhole and she never spoils her dress on the first day. Maman has always had wonderful plans for her: "You just watch," she likes to boast. "Someday, Lily will be involved with world-famous high-fashion houses like Givenchy, Balenciaga, or Jean Patou!"

But what matters most to me is that she swore she would make me a fancy nightgown when I get married.

In addition to enjoying school, Denise writes, Lily belongs to a choir that meets once a week. They have a whole repertoire of songs from the Renaissance, and she loves it.

Good for her! Singing and harmonizing long ago became part of our daily lives. It started in Flers, during the war years in the convent, when a group of Paris children joined us for the summer. We would walk the streets of the town, two by two, all thirty-four of us, to the beat of marching songs. How I loved those walks. Even the sternest of people smiled as we passed by. The lyrics were just as exhilarating as the tunes. They celebrated the beauty of nature and its creator, the splendor of the French countryside, the joys of friendship. I always sang at the top of my voice.

Then one day I stopped short. "How can we sing with such enthusiasm about nature and friendship when such ugly things are being done to the Jews?" I whispered to Denise, marching next to me. She merely pointed to the two nuns walking ahead of us. I knew what she meant. They did risk their lives to save ours! If the Germans ever found out they were hiding Jewish children, they would surely be arrested and killed. So I resumed my singing, determined, in spite of it all, to believe in the basic goodness of humanity.

———

Fernand's letter gives me a day-to-day account of what he does: "I still attend the *cinémathèque* each Thursday evening," he writes, "though I miss not having you at my side. I've seen *Battleship Potemkin* for the third time! And at home, things are pretty much the same."

I can just picture him, sitting at the rectangular dinner table—they have a separate dining room!—facing his brother, Claude; his Uncle Max to his right; his Aunt Ida to his left.

Aunt Ida's flamboyant auburn hair, her imposing silhouette, and the careful way in which she delivers every word give her a distinctive presence. She definitely *tries* to get in a word here and there, but somehow, she only manages to come across as bossy: "Go easy on the salt, Max! You know it's bad for you. That goes for you, too, Fernand!"

My heart always went out to her when she listened to Claude as he painfully stuttered his way through the meal. I could tell how she forced herself *not* to interrupt him or finish a sentence for him. Poor Claude! He was barely four when his father, mother, and older sister were brutally taken away by the Germans that July morning, and that's when he began to stutter.

Actually, Ida confided once, Fernand and Claude were taken along, too, but one of the French policemen who escorted them motioned the boys to get "lost" in a department store along the way, and that's how the two of them escaped.

Regardless, Ida was brave to have taken the two boys—they are Max's sister's sons—into their childless home and to have raised them ever since.

Fernand is a jazz buff. His enthusiasm is really catching. I can't believe I've changed so much in so little time, thanks to him. It's only been a year since we met at the evening class at rue St. André-des-Arts in the Latin Quarter. We liked each other from the start, and he tried from that first night to get me to go with him to the *cinémathèque*. My heart said yes, but my head said no. God knows, I love movies, but why should he ask *me?* I had reasoned. He is so handsome and so sure of himself! Why should he want *me* when Paris is so full of pretty girls more cheerful and less complicated than I am, when all life gave me was thin wrists, a smile with uneven teeth, a musical ear, and a taste for laughter?

I was working as a secretary for a Catholic newspaper, and one day he called me at work to ask me out again. I was so stunned that I said yes.

———

I read and reread his letters. I know them practically by heart. Actually, I'm trying to read between the lines: I'm dying to know who he is dancing with at the jazz club la Huchette on Saturday nights. "I don't dance . . . I'm happy just listening to the music," he writes.

I trust him, of course—at least I *try* to. But I can't get out of my mind the fact that he's quite capable of doing crazy things: Didn't he run off to Palestine to join the Haganah to help fight for the state of Israel? He left one morning without telling his Aunt Ida and Uncle Max. He was barely sixteen years old! He eventually contracted malaria and had to be returned to France.

"How could you leave without telling anyone?" I asked him once, half awed, half admiring.

"That's when I was young and daring—and eager to secure a land for the Jews," he protested.

How can you be angry at a hero?

Still, I can't help wondering: What if he runs out on me one day?

Meanwhile, Fernand wants me to keep my eyes and

ears open for concerts and records. After all, he reminds
me, jazz and all those wonderful musicians come from
America!

He even suggests that I try my hand at ragtime.
Easier said than done!

Monday, February 19

I still live for the mail. I'm spoiled today: I got a letter
from Maman, one from Pépée, and one from Fernand, all
at once!

It's obvious that Maman doesn't like to hear about my
cafard—my feeling homesick and blue.

Instead, she lectures me about how important it is that
I take full advantage of my stay here. And, certainly, I
must be grateful to the Millers for all their efforts.

My friend Pépée is not one for writing any more than
my sister Lily. She must have felt very lonely to fill up
four long pages!

For years, Pépée has been the person I could share
everything with. She is the one who just *knew* when I got
my first kiss. I miss her terribly.

It is sad that in the last year or so before I came to New
York—ever since both of us started to work—we were
unable to visit as often as we wanted to. Her mother,
Mme Larmurier, had become very possessive—even
more than Maman!

"She forbids me to see anyone unless she comes along.
Can you imagine?" Pépée would complain.

Poor Pépée! She has no choice now but to see her

friends on the sly, including the very nice young man she met a few months before I left. She introduced him to me at the Anvers métro station, near where we live. Afterward, on a couple of occasions, she asked me to meet him at the same spot to give him a note because she couldn't get away.

She'll write me as often as she can, she promises. At least she managed to get *this* letter out without her mother catching her.

I only hope that Pépée won't hurry to get married just to run away from home!

Fernand's letter is quite long, too. This coming Saturday, he writes, he expects to attend a political meeting with, he suspects, anti-Semitic overtones. He wants to be there so that he can challenge anyone with such views. He's done this in the past. Every time, I begged him not to.

"Why expose yourself to a bunch of angry, irrational people? Who knows what could happen?" I worried. But he wouldn't listen.

It's strange, I sometimes reflect, that we were both victimized as Jewish children. Yet, we are poles apart in the way we show it today. I, for one, am still hiding. I can't even bring myself to speak of my Jewish background when I *want* to! Twice, in Paris, I braced myself to tell the young ladies I worked with—Geneviève and Madeleine—after I had been invited to their homes. They were so warm and friendly that I wanted to share more about myself with them. Twice, my heart began to race, my palms turned clammy—and my throat choked the words.

But Fernand just *has* to go to those rallies and tell those people how he feels. Sometimes, I wish his confidence would rub off on me. Deep down, I understand him. How can he possibly remain silent when his mother, father, and older sister perished in the camps just because they were Jewish?

He never talks about it. Only once did he show me a letter he received from his sister from the Drancy camp near Paris the day before they were to be put on the train to Auschwitz. You could see the smudges left by the tears on the paper. It brought tears to my eyes, especially the part where she asked Fernand, then ten years old, to take care of his little brother, age four, until they returned.

How can you ever get over that?

I often thought, when I observed Fernand on the sly and wished he would be more careful, of the words of Sister Madeleine, the wise nun I got to like so much, when one of us despaired during the war: "One can't refuse life, my child. One must go on."

All *I* could do was hug Fernand a little harder.

Tuesday, February 27

I'm glad I don't have to bother with the telephone.

Rita can't imagine how people can live without one. She can't go a single day without chatting with Sally and Candy, even when she's *seen* them in the afternoon.

This evening, as usual, Adele monopolizes the telephone after dinner. She often chats with her friend Judy Rudman, while I softly play some easy pieces on the piano, trying not to disturb her.

Adele has hardly ended her chat with Judy when the phone rings again.

"I'll get it!" Rita says, dashing to pick it up.

"Renée, it's for you," she announces.

"For me?" I question, getting up from the piano bench. "Someone who speaks English?"

Her smile puzzles me. Who could it be? I don't know a soul here!

"Here," she insists, handing me the receiver. "It *is* for you!"

"*Allo?*" I venture timidly, my heart racing.

"*Allo!* Renée?" I sigh with relief. Somebody is addressing me in French.

"It's Giza, Adele's sister. Welcome to New York."

"Thank you."

"It's so wonderful to have you here! My son, Joseph, is also looking forward to meeting you, to have someone to speak French to! You'll have to come to visit us. But we live all the way in the Bronx. In the meantime, maybe we can meet for coffee somewhere in town?"

"That would be nice. Thank you," I reply.

"Fine. We'll arrange that. *A bientôt*—see you soon!"

"*A bientôt!*"

I am walking on air by the time I return to the piano bench.

I think I have a friend!

———

I wake up with a start. I have had a dream. For a moment, it feels so real that my chest is pounding, I am fighting a sense of doom. In the dream, I am in a phone booth. I have dialed the number and reached the desired party, but he can't hear me. I speak louder, I shout, because he is the doctor and we can't waste any more time:

Papa has suddenly taken very ill. I know I am still struggling with what happened that evening in December of 1946.

Papa has become short of breath while getting ready for bed. It is after ten o'clock. I am still up, studying for a test in school the next day. Both my sisters are asleep in the back bedroom.

"Go down and call the police. Quick!" Maman urges me as she opens the window to give Papa more air. "We need an ambulance. Hurry!"

I throw my coat over my pajamas, get into my shoes, and rush down the five flights to the glass pole at the street corner that must be broken to call the local police precinct.

I speak into it. I scream into it. To no avail. It is out of order.

Please God! Keep Papa alive! I plead, frantic by now, rushing to the Café Redon to phone Dr. Diamond, the family doctor, grateful that the café is still open at that late hour.

The doctor's wife answers: "Sorry, my husband can't possibly make any housecalls. He's in bed with the flu."

I beg, I cry, I ask to speak to Dr. Diamond himself. But his wife is adamant. I look at the receiver, angry at this heartless lady on the other end of the line, and smash it down on its base.

I am hysterical by the time I climb the five flights to ask Maman what to do next. M. Chavignat, our neighbor, has been alerted and is at my mother's side.

"Just go to Dr. Diamond's home and force him out of bed!" she decides. "Don't pay any attention to his wife! Go ahead!" she adds, motioning me to the door.

"I'm coming along," M. Chavignat offers.

We run the few blocks in the dark, frigid night. I am not even aware of the cold. I am shaking, moaning, praying frantically, "Please, God! Keep Papa alive until the doctor gets there!" grateful for M. Chavignat's presence.

We finally get the doctor to come with us—a feat in itself.

"Let's hurry! Please!" I beg the man, pulling him forward by the sleeve all the endless mile home.

I hear Maman's heartbreaking moans from the staircase. I know it is too late.

II

SPRING

SPRING 1951

Sunday, March 11

I am getting a glimpse of New York beyond Tompkins Square and the Millers'. We have just come from visiting the Rudmans, and now Stanley insists on showing me Broadway and Times Square on the way home.

The Rudmans—Judy and Herb, as they were introduced to me—were warm and friendly. I still have a hard time addressing older people by their first names. In France, you address people as Monsieur or Madame, whether you know them casually or have known them all your life.

I felt immediately at home, as I do whenever I enter a

Jewish household. There I can be myself and not worry about giving myself away. "There's nothing like being among your own people!" Maman often said, she who always saw the world in black and white: that which is Jewish and that which is not.

"We finally get to meet you!" Judy exclaimed. She was wonderfully thin in her red outfit, her dark hair pulled back in a ponytail.

"*Finally* is right!" echoed Herb, baldish and chunky.

The area of Brooklyn where the Rudmans live is quite charming, with quiet, tree-lined streets and quaint three- or four-story townhouses—a different world altogether from Tompkins Square.

We all took a walk on the Promenade, overlooking the river separating Brooklyn from Manhattan. There was that striking skyline again, with those awesome skyscrapers that are breathtaking no matter at what angle you catch them. The low clouds, the peculiar light of the late afternoon, made it almost eerie. How I wished I had a camera to capture that sight so that I could send a photo to Fernand, my sisters, and Pépée. It would describe it better than words.

"Well, how do you like America?" a voice asked behind me. It was Herb's.

How does one answer, in one sentence or less, such a question? One can't. I would have to explain that there are many wonderful things in this country that I would appreciate much better if I weren't homesick and lonely. But Herb was eager for an answer.

"Do you mean America or New York?" I asked finally.

"Touché!" He laughed.

I laughed, too. "Ask me again later—when I can explain better," I said.

=====

So now we are on our way to Times Square.

"There's nothing like it anywhere," Stanley says. "It's probably the only place in the world where you can eat at any time of the day or night, or get a haircut at two in the morning!"

I had certainly heard about Broadway, with its musical shows and theaters—even our Yves Montand sings about the *petit cireurs de Broadway*—the little shoeshine boys of Broadway.

Is this *it*? I ask myself, facing gigantic billboards, flickering neon signs, moving screens delivering the latest news, the rather ordinary theaters. I'm not sure what I expected: a more glamorous scene, with elegant women walking down Broadway in glittering slinky dresses and elegant cigar-smoking men riding down in the latest-model cars. . . . Maybe I am confusing Broadway with Hollywood?

"Well, what do you think?" both Adele and Rita ask me. Their eyes are riveted on me with such expectation!

"It's *different*," I concede. Then I exclaim, "Now *that's* interesting," pointing to the larger-than-life Camel man in the distance smoking a cigarette and releasing huge smoke rings into the air.

But most interesting to me are the crowds of people walking about: men and women in flashy outfits, carrying on in loud voices, strolling alongside average-looking persons—obviously tourists—stopping at the brightly lit shop windows or gathering in small groups to smile at flashing cameras.

Someone taps me on the shoulder. I swing my head around: A youngish man is handing me a camera and, pointing to two children and an adult, motions me to take a snapshot. "Please?"

I nod an enthusiastic "Of course!" while he dashes to join the threesome.

Obviously, he is a tourist who doesn't speak English. He must have taken me for a New Yorker!

As I gladly oblige, I am keenly aware that I am living a magic moment, and that I am treading the ground of a world-famous legendary spot, where the fantastic meets the ordinary.

Wednesday, March 28

There is still more to see, I learn, and today, Giza Rosen, Adele's sister, is taking me to Macy's, the largest department store in the world!

I've seen Giza twice. Once we met in a coffee shop in town, and then she invited me to lunch last Sunday at her apartment in the Bronx, where I also met her husband, Simon, and their son, Joseph.

"I would love for you to visit us every Sunday," she said. "But I don't want to take you away from Adele."

I would enjoy this, too, although I'm not too keen on riding the subway to the Bronx alone. It was a memorable experience: I tried to overlook the bleak walls and the chipped paint and the noise. The train was so long you couldn't see the end of it. And I kept my impressions to myself. I could just hear what Adele would have retorted: "The subway got you there, didn't it? And fast,

too!" No doubt about that! The train shook all the way;
I was afraid it would jump off the tracks a hundred times.

At last, we are nearing Macy's. I glance at Giza as we
walk arm in arm, just as I would walk with my sisters or
my friends in Paris. She is so different from Adele: casual,
with little makeup, her graying hair pulled back in a bun.
She is wearing a plain tweed coat and flat shoes. She is
kind and warm—and not a gossip.

"We are sisters," she had commented simply when we
first met, referring to Adele, setting things straight from
the start. "And, though we don't always see eye to eye,
we try to get along."

Her French is a bit rusty, but she understands everything. Actually, I can't wait to talk to her, now. It is as if
the emotion and excitement I must constantly contain
when I express myself in English gush out whenever I
speak to her. She is familiar with life in Paris—she lived
on Faubourg-St. Antoine for several years.

"How was your life before Paris—in Alsace, I mean?"
Giza asks. "Did you live in a big town?"

I tell her of the carefree summers in Mulhouse, the
rides in the open streetcars to the beach of the River Ill or
to our famed zoo, Papa's card games at the Café de la
Republique.

"Seems to me you're only remembering the *good*
days," she remarks softly. "Surely, there were also air
raids and those awful gas masks you mentioned the other
day? And don't forget, you were *forced* out of your hometown, *forced* to leave a home you loved!"

I looked at her, stunned. She is right. Images drift
across my mind—my saying good-bye, with tears in my
voice, to every milestone, every village. Yet, whenever I
visualize my early youth, it is *always* carefree and sunny.

In spite of the disruptions that shattered my life, the world of my childhood *does* live within me—more so now, it seems, that I need to hold on to it to make my way in an unfamiliar world. A whiff of cinnamon in the air throws me back to my mother's prewar baking days. The mere mention of a Parisian street or of a certain town in Normandy or Alsace, or even a few tremolos of an accordion, shoot a painful longing through me. And memories return. . . .

I can barely contain myself as I am boarding the train with Papa at gare de l'Est. It is my first trip by train since the war ended a year and a half ago.

I always liked the hustle-bustle of train stations, the shared excitement of those leaving, of those remaining—a last embrace, a last kiss, a lingering look while the conductor's whistle announces the last call. "Everyone aboard!" our conductor thunders.

"Careful with your suitcase!" Maman urges from the platform.

I'm standing by the open window now, as the train is picking up speed, with Papa next to me, waving good-bye to Maman, Denise, and Lily. They are waving back, growing farther away and smaller until they vanish from sight.

This is my first trip back to Alsace after an exile of six years. Alsace—the mere word evokes magic for me: the stork nests, our carefree summers in a little cottage on the banks of the River Thur, the neighbor's son playing the accordion every evening, our outings to the mountaintop Hartsmannswillerkopf.

"Eh, bien, ma grande," Papa says. "We have a long trip ahead of us."

Funny, I think to myself. These are the same exact words he spoke last time we traveled together—when the two of us, flee-ing Alsace, walked across the Vosges Mountains because there was no room in the military van that took my mother, grand-mother, and sisters to safety.

He lets me sit by the window. There are only three other passengers in our compartment: an elderly gentleman sitting across from me—I'm not sure whether he is dozing off or just pretending—and two middle-aged ladies. One of them has taken out her knitting in spite of the dimming light—the sun is setting. The other one is trying to read a book.

There is no attempt at conversation—just a polite greeting when we entered the compartment. There is no hurry. We won't get to Mulhouse, three hundred miles away, for another ten hours.

I look at Papa reading his France-Soir. *His shoulders look more stooped, his hair more sparse, the furrows on his face more pronounced. He is tired and, for the first time, I see how he has aged. I prefer to look away.*

How odd! I tell myself. For the longest time, I was convinced that Papa didn't really love me—well, not quite the way he loved Denise. He and Maman always carry on so about how efficient and sensible Denise is. And certainly, he never fussed over me the way he fussed over Lily, who is so clever with her hands and had seemed to be his favorite as far back as I can remember.

I began to change my mind the day he took a firm stand against Maman, who had taken to nagging me nonstop—be-cause I listened to the radio much too late into the night, because I preferred to play the piano before settling down to do my homework, because . . . because.

"Let her be, for God's sake!" Papa finally said. And then one night, he announced, "I'm taking Renée to Alsace. Fanny and Maurice have been wanting us to visit them for months.

63

She's been working extra hard in school and needs to get away for a bit. We'll go for a week during Easter recess."

"What about us?" Denise and Lily asked in one voice.

"You'll go another time."

I couldn't believe my luck. For once, it paid to be the oldest!

"We should be getting to the Mulhouse station sometime after six in the morning," Papa whispers, emerging from behind his newspaper. "There will be enough time to have a café crème before catching the Flèche Bleue *bus to Guebwiller."*

Flèche Bleue—*"blue arrow"—the name of the bus that we rode so many times. Guebwiller, the pretty, quiet little town at the foot of the mountain by the same name. It all comes back. I was not quite nine when we left, but I recall the bus driver greeting the passengers as they boarded the bus, as if he knew them personally, and announcing very loudly in Alsatian the names of the little towns we crossed on the way to Guebwiller: Bollviller, Wittenheim, Pulversheim. At Soultz—the stop before my aunt and uncle's town—I would get all nervous and excited in anticipation of seeing the family again.*

I hope we'll get to stop in Mulhouse, too, so I can see our street and our apartment on the second floor, with its balcony overlooking our narrow garden. I have mixed feelings about going back. I've grown to love Paris and the school and the friends I've made. But then, no spot in the world ever takes the place of one's hometown!

It is dark in our compartment now. Papa is resting against the hard wooden back of the seat, his head slightly to the side. One of the ladies has dozed off, her hand still holding her knitting needles; the other is in a deep sleep, her mouth open, and snores ever so slightly.

I feel secure and comfortable, but I can't sleep. I am too excited. The train has stopped. I look through the window. We are in Troyes, about a quarter of the way. Outside, the night is

64

pitch black. There's only one light, in the middle of the plat-form. A handful of people get off. "Hello, Troyes!" I whisper.

A long whistle, and the train starts again. The next stop is Bar-sur-Aube, then Chaumont. As I watch the bleak, stark landscape whip by, I am tempted to say hello to every passing village, just the way I said good-bye to every milestone when we left Alsace, wondering if we were leaving never to return.

I settle on the wooden bench next to Papa, trying to find some sleep. I must be rested tomorrow—and ready for the big day.

I wake up with a start and wipe the sleep out of my eyes. I must have dozed off. I hear voices outside our compartment, in the long corridor running through the train.

My companions, Papa included, are still asleep. I get up quietly and tiptoe to the corridor. I slide the door open and close it behind me.

The voices are closer and clearer. There are only two people in the corridor, both uniformed conductors. They are speaking to each other in Alsatian, a language I haven't heard spoken for more than six years.

Before I can stop them, my eyes brim with tears.

"What's the matter, mademoiselle?" one of the conductors asks.

"I'm going home!" I want to explain, but the words get strangled in my throat.

All I can do is smile apologetically and dash back to my seat. Everyone is still asleep. I settle down as if nothing happened. No one has to know, I think to myself.

This is strictly between Alsace and me.

"Don't *you* ever get homesick? Don't you ever miss Vienna?" I wonder aloud now to Giza.

I don't want to hear that she doesn't, that you get over it in time.

Giza doesn't get to answer my question.

"We are here! This is Macy's!" she proclaims, bringing me back to reality. We are at Thirty-fourth Street and Broadway, a corner as densely packed as any Paris street on market day, with nothing but stores on both sides of the street.

"Which way do we get in?" I ask.

"Anywhere we can! It's a whole block long and nine stories high," Giza informs me, not without a tinge of pride.

We literally push our way in.

I can't help being impressed by the wide spaces, the easy access to the various counters. I've always liked department stores. Just as I did in the Galeries Lafayette or the Bon Marché, I find myself gravitating toward the cosmetics counters. Here, as in Paris, impeccably groomed young ladies try to convince the hesitant customers that miracle lotions will make the skin glow, the eyelashes thick, and wrinkles disappear. I take in the heady fragrances that float about and make me feel rich and sophisticated.

"May I try this new perfume on you?" a young lady calls out to us, an elegant atomizer dangling from her hand.

"No . . . no, thank you!" I mutter with an apologetic smile. "Maybe another time!"

Giza pulls me away. "Come on," she whispers. "Let's go before she talks us into buying something we don't want—and certainly don't need!"

The saleslady has now turned to a co-worker on the far side of the counter.

"Hey, Carol," I hear her ask loudly, "how was your

seder last night?" The voice is clear. The word unmistakable.

I gasp. My heart is pounding. I want to hide. I look around for some reaction from the people milling past, who must have heard it just as I did. How can they—how can anyone—be talking so openly about the seder, a Jewish ritual? I wonder to myself in disbelief.

To my astonished eyes, it is business as usual. The customers continue their idle walk, the salesladies their chat. How wonderful it must be not to feel shame!

Slowly, something in me begins to break free.

Did you hear that? I want to ask Giza. But the words get stuck in my throat. Instead, I strain to smile—a wide, extended smile that forces the tears back in.

Wednesday, April 4

I lie awake in my bed, savoring this moment of quiet, cozy privacy in Murray's room—now mine—waiting for the buzz of the alarm to signal the beginning of the day. I can't help thinking of my sisters back in Paris. Our bedroom was so frigid during the winter months that we'd dress and undress under the covers.

Cold, to me, is even harder to endure than hunger. Sometimes Maman and Lily accused me of being too much of a *douilette*—a softie. It's easy for them to say! They're always too hot and run around in short sleeves. Fernand is the only one who understands me. Did he ever realize, I wonder, that the very first time he really found the way to my heart was on that cold, windy night, when

67

he casually stopped to rearrange my scarf and raised the collar of my coat without a word, as if it were the most natural gesture in the world. Or that he completely won me over a couple of weeks later when, in a poorly heated movie theater where we had finally settled after two hours of waiting in line and stomping our feet in the cold, he did this incredible thing: He took off his socks in the dark and gave them to me to wear over mine.

I miss him terribly. I miss the way his eyes tell me that everything will be all right, the warmth and tenderness he unlocks in me as he holds my face in his hands, the fact that I can tell him *most* of what bothers me and that he hears me between the lines.

I love Fernand so, and yet it's hard for me to say "I love you." The words seem so trite, so worn. Every dime novel, every song, proclaims them. Of course, I show my love in many ways. Didn't I go down each of the twelve avenues that radiate from the place de l'Etoile to find him among thousands gathered at a military parade? Still I wish it were easier to say what I feel.

Fernand isn't that vocal, either. But I know he loves me, too; his hand in my hair says it, his quarter smile, which only I can detect, says it. His saying "Here!" whenever I need him says it.

The main connection between two human beings, one that doesn't fool anyone and needs no words, is laughter. And the two of us laugh together an awful lot.

At least now, in writing letters, I can express those feelings that I was too shy to express verbally. By the time I return to France, Fernand will know all my secrets.

Feelings have an odd way of showing through, though, when you least expect it. As I was tucking Rita in last night, I was all set to try, in English, the "Good-night, honey" I heard so often on TV. What came out, instead, was *"Bonsoir, ma puce,"*—my little flea—an affectionate pet name I would use for my sisters or friends. What it told me, of course, is how fond I am of Rita.

"I like to hear you speak French." Rita smiled. "Your voice is different; you're much more lively."

No doubt about it. Learning a new language is like learning to fit into new clothes, and it takes time getting used to wearing them. Words! Words! Words! I'm not merely learning a new language, I'm finding out a lot about myself. It's hard to believe, but I find it easier to show—and express—frustration and anger in English!

═════

The radio clock goes off.

Time to get up!

Friday, April 6

I am ironing while listening to the radio. I love to iron—turning a wet, rumpled piece of rag into a smooth, fresh-smelling garment.

And I love to listen to the radio. It has been my favorite possession ever since Jews were permitted to own radios again after the war. In Paris, I used to stay up until the wee hours of the morning listening to the music from cities far away.

They're playing one of my favorite songs, a rhumba, *"Si vous m'aimiez autant que je vous aime,"* but the lyrics are in Spanish. *"Tres palabras."* I rest the iron on the board and begin to dance.

It's strange how a tune can evoke memories. I close my eyes, and there I am, on the dance floor of l'Hôtel Lutetia, dancing with Fernand.

Different tunes remind me of different occasions. Whenever they play *"Cerisiers roses et pommiers blancs"* ("Cherry Pink and Apple Blossom White"), I think of the first Bastille Day after the war, when Parisians were delirious with joy and danced in the streets three nights in a row. I had walked with my sisters and some neighbors to the Faubourg Poissonière. All traffic had stopped. A small band was set right in the middle of the Faubourg. That's where I heard for the first time *"Cerisiers roses et pommiers blancs"* and fell in love with the song. We danced nonstop all night.

This was also the Bastille Day of the year my father died.

Oddly enough, no song comes to mind when I think of him—except for the lullaby he sang to my sisters and me when we were very small, and that was in Polish!

I wonder what song I will take back from America?

Adele is home. I didn't expect her yet. She has been out quite late these past few days, so we haven't had our usual chat while preparing dinner in the late afternoon.

Adele brings out the potatoes and dumps them onto the kitchen counter, where we are now both standing, and hands me a knife—without a word. We begin to peel. Something is up: She is using the paring knife in very slow, hesitating motions.

Actually, I've been expecting her to want to talk to me ever since I received a note from Murray. He is in basic training somewhere in New Jersey.

"It was nice of Murray to write you a note, don't you think?" she finally asks.

"Yes. Quite nice," I agree, cautious.

"If you want my opinion, I think Murray really likes you."

I stop, staring at the spiral dangling on my knife, and then look at her. "I guess he does," I reply. "And so do Rita and Stanley—and you!" I add, trying to diffuse the issue.

"Of course we're *all* very fond of you. You're a *sympathique,* bright, responsible girl. Why do you think I wanted you to come to New York?"

She pauses and rests her knife on the edge of the table. Her eyes lock mine. "Remember when we first met, a few years ago? What were the first words I said to you? That I liked you and thought of you as a girlfriend for my son—and possibly a daughter-in-law, some day."

"I remember. It was very flattering. But I was not even sixteen. How could I take it seriously? So many things have happened to me since—like meeting Fernand."

"I'm aware of that. But he is so young. Besides, he hasn't got a *real* profession, and he hasn't even been in the military yet. At least that's what your mother says."

That is *our* business! I want to snap. But, instead, I turn my attention to the potato and continue to peel furiously. Now I have *two* mothers ganging up against me. My own, miles away, and Adele.

Fernand and I have never discussed the future. But I just can't imagine a life without him. Besides, the mere thought of settling here permanently—away from the people I know and love and my familiar world—is unthinkable.

I take a deep breath and, having regained my composure, I speak again. "You know how much I appreciate all you've done for me, Adele. And I'm honored that you'd want me in your family. But I am very much attached to Fernand and, as far as I can tell, Murray is quite taken by Evelyn, so there's really nothing to talk about, is there?

"Besides," I add quickly, wanting to get it all out before she silences me. "Paris *is* my home!"

"Look, Renée," Adele says, her voice a bit softer. "Of course Paris is beautiful. I go there every time I get a chance. But who can afford to live there?"

She pauses a moment and then adds, enunciating every word slowly for emphasis, her eyes darkening, "Just tell me: How often have you been able to afford a new coat or a new dress? And when is the last time when you sat on the terrace of a café?"

So what? I want to snap back. People live out their lives in Paris just as they do here! But there's no point in pursuing the argument, I decide.

She must have read the pain on my face, as she reaches across the table for my hand. "I know you love Fernand," she concedes. "But you'll get over it, just as Murray will get over Evelyn, believe me! I was not in love with Stanley when I married him. We were introduced. That's the way it was done in the old days, and still is in many areas of the world. . . . It's a sensible way to get together people who would not meet otherwise."

She is talking about matchmaking! I'm neither that old nor that desperate! I rage silently, grabbing the potato and cutting an angry slab out of it. What's more, she, of all people, should know how that can fail!

"I bet your parents were introduced, too," Adele continues, relentless.

They were *not*! I almost shout, though now I can't really swear to that. The couple of snapshots my mother has left of their courting days show a happy twosome—happy enough to warrant that the pairing-off was a much wanted one.

"Look, Adele," I conclude with a firmness I didn't know I had. "I'll answer Murray's note—that's all it is, a friendly *note*—as I would anyone else's. I love Fernand and I hope we will marry some day. That's all I can say for now. It makes it so much easier when two people come from similar backgrounds, speak the same language, anyway."

"Nonsense!" Adele snaps. "That's no guarantee! Don't kid yourself. Just think for a moment: When two people have both had a troubled childhood, they're *both* likely to be more sensitive and easily hurt and they're likely to have a more difficult time in a marriage no matter how much in love they are!"

But wouldn't two people with different backgrounds not see eye to eye and have different expectations—and get into difficulty just the same? I protest silently, determined not to argue a losing battle.

"Look," Adele concludes, "I just want you to think about it. Let's drop the subject for now and keep it to ourselves."

Later in the evening, when the dishes are done and everything is quiet, I try to remember. What is it in Adele that won me over the moment I first met her in Paris? She was, I guess, everything my mother wasn't: She paid a great deal of attention to her appearance. She was cheerful and positive about life. She didn't seem weighed down by the responsibilities of a home and children and was always involved in some new, exciting project. And, of course, she fussed over me: She admired my flair for clothes and colors, loved the way I played the piano, and always commented on how serious and responsible I was.

I couldn't remember when Maman last had something nice to say about what I said or did.

It is clear to me now: It is a mother I looked for in Adele!

But Adele is *not* my mother, I now must admit that. She is probably the last one to suspect that I need one! And why should anyone think I still need a mother, when I'm old enough to have a boyfriend, a job, when I surely must be mature to have crossed the Atlantic to live in a foreign country and take care of someone else's child?

I must face it! Adele wasn't concerned about *me*. All she wanted was someone reliable to watch over her daughter and help her around the house, and perhaps to make a nice, dutiful, Jewish wife for her son.

I feel betrayed and abandoned. I don't know where to hide, so I rush to the bathroom, where I take a long shower to drown my tears and cover up my sobs, unable to stop the rush of the cry: "Maman! Maman!" The water is warm and soothing, I don't want it to stop. Why do I cry now for my mother miles away, when she doesn't even hear me when I'm next to her?

———

Later, when I'm in bed, I'm too upset to sleep.

I throw off the sheet and the blanket, step into my slippers, and walk to the window. The buildings across the yard are quiet and dark. The sky above is of a deep navy blue and is twinkling with stars.

I miss my father. I need to speak to Papa, and look for him somewhere among the stars. I want to tell him about so many things: the kind of music I like, my love for dancing, and especially my feelings for Fernand. And I wish I could tell him about my troubles, too.

In his last few years, Papa really came to appreciate my efforts in school, down to the night he died, when I had stayed up late to prepare for a test the next day.

"When you graduate, we'll go to Nice, just you and me!" he had vowed.

I so looked forward to it! I had never seen the Mediterranean, or any ocean for that matter.

I never got a chance to tell him that I was sorry I didn't know that he had loved me all those years—he who so wanted a boy!

For months after his death, I couldn't look at a snapshot of him. How heartbreaking it was to hold the shirt he wore or the hat he sometimes used to cover his Star of David during the war. How unbearable to know that he would never again dip his *petit beurre* cookies into his *café au lait*.

It's getting harder to remember him.

His voice went first, and then his smile.

All that remains is his nose and his hat.

=====

Moved by the silence and the darkness, I hum to myself: "*O Nuit, qu'il est profond ton silence,*" the song by Rameau praising the night as a serene, protective blanket.

Tears come to my eyes, and I am again in the barn in Normandy. We are singing, all twenty-five of us, the evening air still because the shelling has come to a full stop. We are settling for the night, yet still facing the unknown, and we are singing at the top of our voices, to keep from crying or from dying of fear.

It always did the trick—and still does.

When I die, many years from now, this is the tune I would want to hear last.

Saturday, April 7

It is Saturday. The day goes on forever. There's no school, and everything is more leisurely: Adele went to her regular hairdresser's appointment, after which she will go shopping with her friend Judy. Rita lingered in bed and got up just in time to be picked up by Candy's mother, who took both girls to their weekly ballet class.

Stanley is home. He's keeping me company while I tidy up the kitchen, reading his *Daily Mirror,* sipping his third cup of coffee.

There's no mail from France today. Of course; I'm forgotten again. Life continues in Paris without me. Denise wrote that she bumped into Fernand on boulevard Saint-Germain. He was with a bunch of friends—including a girl. What if it was pretty Sarah? I ask myself with increasing anguish—a born dancer and a charmer, who hangs around the jazz club on Friday and Saturday nights?

How I hated Maman's planting doubts in my mind when she remarked before I left:

"You can't trust men, believe me! What do you think Fernand will do while you're gone? Stay home?"

Where on earth did she dig up such ideas, I had wondered. Wasn't Papa the only man in her life?

Stanley's laughter interrupts my thoughts. He's got a loud, almost childish laugh. He must be reading the comics—he just *loves* the comic strips.

"Renée, come here! I want you to look at this!"

I walk toward him and look at the cartoon. I smile politely. But I just can't see what's funny about the picture he shows me.

"Don't feel bad. . . . It's silly of me to expect you to understand. Every language, every country has got its own brand of humor. It's the last thing you learn—and you can't explain it!

"What's the matter? No mail today?" Stanley teases. He must have sensed my restlessness. "Come on, Renée. . . . You just can't go on waiting for the mail and wishing your life away! It's a nice day out. Why don't you take the afternoon off and walk around the neighborhood. Here," he adds, reaching for his wallet and handing me five singles. "Treat yourself to something nice. Don't worry about Rita—I'll be here when she returns. I've got a bunch of swatches to go over and I've got to get my bills ready for the taxes; they must be paid by the fifteenth of this month!"

It feels somewhat uncomfortable taking the money. But the eighty dollars I brought with me from Paris are nearly spent, and there's been no money coming in during the three months I've been here. The subject was never discussed—Maman was so grateful to see me go to America after the long waiting, and I just never dared ask Adele about being paid. Maybe Stanley is the person to ask—but not now.

"Thank you!" I exclaim, throwing my arms around him and kissing him spontaneously on the cheek.

It *is* a good idea, and I get ready in no time. I put on

77

some lipstick, get into my coat, and rush out the door before I change my mind.

The April air is warm and pleasant. No more rushing and bundling up to protect myself from the sharp winter wind. The promise of spring hangs in the air: new fragrances, the new stirrings in Tompkins Square, with tiny buds popping all over the bare trees and the birds chirping with renewed vigor. My mind flicks back to Paris—will it always?—where, too, spring means the warming of the sun, but also the return of the lilacs and the strawberries. And, of course, the offering of lilies of the valley to all the loved ones on the first of May.

I am brimming with an irrepressible force and I want to stretch after the long, numbing winter. I wish I had a favorite spot here—a bunch of trees, a riverbank—that I could watch coming to life again. I walk bouncily along Avenue A, feeling a rush of tenderness toward the passersby: the young mother battling with her reluctant toddler, the elderly lady counting the change in her palm to give the newspaperman, two middle-aged women looking strikingly alike—twins, no doubt—walking with arms locked, chatting happily.

Stanley is right: I can't spend every waking hour thinking of back home. There's a whole world out here, too.

At least here, these straight, angular, look-alike streets are empty of memories.

I'm not reminded, as I was in Paris, whenever I walked past rue du Delta, where the Jaffes and the Rosenbergs lived, or turned onto rue de Bellefond, where Feigie lived, or crossed boulevard de Sebastopol, where we had visited the Kleins and the Schriffts many a Sunday afternoon, that no one would ever return to ring their bells, and if anyone did, no one familiar would answer. There are now big voids where there once were laughter and faces lighting up at the sight of the soup being served around the dimly lit table.

———

I stop at Woolworth and decide to be extravagant: I treat myself to two lipsticks, a red-orange and a "rose bonbon." Then I decide to treat myself to a movie.

Movies are, I discovered, the best way to fight loneliness in this big New York. They beat wandering aimlessly in the streets, milling with the indifferent crowd, or passing by a phone booth and wondering whom to call. You get to feel and live with the characters portrayed on the screen, and you forget everything.

Still, I can't get excited about some of the programs they show on TV. "What's the matter, Renée? Don't you like to watch a good story?" Adele unfailingly remarks when she sees me leave the living room.

How can I explain that I have little in common with the people on the TV screen—that pretty lady with the perfect smile, or that other character, dressed in the latest fashion and always chipper, as if she didn't have a worry in the world? I'd rather watch a tired man in baggy pants and a rumpled jacket rolling up a cigarette—like the movie actors Raimu or Fernandel at home—or a bunch of ordinary folks arguing over a card game in the shabby back room of a café, or even a friendship evolve between two people, shown merely by their gestures and the expressions on their faces. I like to see the stuff of everyday life and how people survive.

That's why I so admire Charlie Chaplin—Charlot, as we affectionately call him in France. There's such poignancy and eloquence in his face, in his peculiar walk and the way he thrashes his cane about, in his clumsy and desperate attempts to remain a gentleman while trying to wiggle himself out of the worst snags. And especially the way he walks off, straight ahead after it is all over, with his hat and cane, ready for the next venture.

But today, something wonderful happens. What started out as a sad day suddenly holds all sorts of wonders for me. Today, for the first time, I really appreciate an American movie. I am suddenly more aware of the nuances of the language—the hesitations, the changes in the voices, the facial expressions—because I no longer strain to follow the dialogue. Today, I see Bette Davis and Errol Flynn, as Queen Elizabeth I and Essex, and it is a revelation. I saw Errol Flynn in a movie in Paris, but all I remember is how handsome he was. This time, I don't miss a thing: the way he looks at Bette Davis, the way he actually flirts with her. I love just as much Bette's reactions, her jerky movements, her haughtiness. I *feel* the bond between them.

I end my afternoon at Horn and Hardart, having a cup of coffee.

As I am sitting alone at a table near the window, I notice a frail woman at the next table. She has a worn, faded dress. She looks worn, too: graying wisps hang down sadly from the combs holding back her hair. Her hand is clutching the cup as if to keep warm, outside and inside.

But what gets to me are the deep wrinkles in her face. Many sorrows must have put them there! I feel a rush of tenderness for this fellow sufferer. How long has she been sitting here? Is there someone waiting for her at home to tell her she has a fine, sensitive face?

I now observe, sitting at the table in back of her, an elderly gentleman, an empty plate in front of him. He hasn't even taken the trouble of removing his hat. He is picking his teeth, looking vacantly ahead of him.

If I had my way, I would sit them across from each other.

I'm grateful for no longer feeling so alone in this big city. I gulp down my coffee and leave like a thief.

======

After dinner, I keep a promise I made to myself. I stick around to watch "Your Show of Shows." Stanley and Adele are sitting on the sofa next to me. Rita is sprawled on the floor in front of the set. I've watched fragments of this variety show before—mostly musical numbers or spoofs of old films.

Something is suddenly catching my attention: the way the man on the screen constantly adjusts the knot of his tie, straightens the hanky in his pocket, and smoothes over his hair with his hand, his face ridden by tics! That man *knows* what it is to be nervous!

There is something of the poignancy of Charlie Chaplin's little tramp in this tall, sturdy Sid Caesar. He is vulnerable. As he gets more anxious, his tics multiply. He is in constant motion. He has become such a mess that he is hilarious. Stanley is roaring. Rita and Adele are glued to the screen.

I can't believe what I see next. Sid Caesar begins portraying a professor of some sort. He's got a rumpled hat, his baggy clothes hang over him—echoes of Charlot again. He speaks with a marked German accent, even I can detect it. He is being interviewed by Carl Reiner who, I could swear, has a hard time keeping a straight face.

Something is happening within me. My eyes and ears are riveted on every word that comes out of Sid Caesar's mouth as he carries on his deadpan dialogue with Carl Reiner. I hear him say *chutzpah, shah,* and *schmaltz,* words I knew years ago. Is it possible? This man is speaking Yiddish words! Right in the open, addressing and entertaining millions of television viewers!

Before long, I am shaking and rocking and coughing with laughter—laughing at him, at myself. And then I burst into uncontrollable sobs; liberating, long overdue sobs.

Tuesday, April 24

The whole household is bubbling with excitement: Murray will be spending his last night with us. He's finished his training and is leaving tomorrow. He just got his orders. He's being shipped to an American base in Germany. At least he's not being sent to Korea, and his parents wanted to see him, before he left, to celebrate that good news. The best he could do, he said to Adele, was to get here late tonight and say good-bye in the morning.

Murray will of course sleep in his room. So here I am, relegated once again to the living-room sofa.

It is past midnight. The lights are out. Everyone is asleep—except me. There's no telling when Murray will come home. He was to spend a couple of hours with Evelyn and her family and then get together with some fellow recruits for a last bash. The plan is to have a festive breakfast—brunch *en famille* tomorrow.

There's a sound at the front door. Someone is putting the key into the lock. I keep my eyes shut, facing the wall, pretending to be asleep. I hope that Murray is very tired and will tiptoe past me into his room.

I don't hear any footsteps. Wondering what's going on, I turn my head ever so slightly and find—God help me!—Murray's face so close to mine that I can only surmise that he was going to kiss me. And his hand has reached my leg under the cover!

Caught in a panic, I scream, "What are you doing?" and push him away with all my might. Some instinct prompts me to hit the piano keys blessedly within reach of my arm.

"Why all that noise?" Murray asks, laughing. "All I wanted was to kiss you good-night!"

Only now do I notice his uniform and a closely cropped haircut. Ironically, his neatly pressed shirt, the well-fitted uniform, the gold letters on his lapel give him a serious, respectable demeanor.

Soon Adele shows up in her pink satin nightgown. Her initial startled look quickly gives way to a smile as Stanley and Rita walk into the living room.

She understood! I tell myself. I *know* it! I *feel* it!

"Sorry to have awakened you all," I apologize, still flushed and shaky. "I panicked in the dark and I hit the keyboard," I explain, as evenly as I can, sitting upright on the sofa now, deliberately avoiding Murray's eyes.

"Do you know that it's close to two o'clock in the morning? Let's open the champagne right now, since we're all up!" Adele suggests.

Only once do I meet Murray's eyes—when he raises his drink for the toast. He winks at me—as he would at an accomplice! He's hopeless!

I *am* grateful for the piano.

And for Murray's departure tomorrow!

The apartment is quiet again; the lights are out. It is past three in the morning, but my eyes are wide open, my mind brimming with thoughts. I can't help being reminded of the homecoming of another soldier. It was when my cousin Paul came back into our lives with a bang. . . .

My sisters and I have only been back from Normandy a few days. The air is full of excitement. Parisians are still celebrating their newly acquired freedom as the victorious Allies march in and push the Germans out.

Parisians are smiling again, crying with joy, denouncing those sales boches—*dirty Germans—who are finally getting what they deserve. Photos of General de Gaulle and the French flag have come out of hiding and decorate many a window. The war is not over yet, but we are well on our way.*

My parents, my sisters, and I are sitting around the dining-room table—we always seem to be sitting around the table when important things happen. The bell rings, and in walks a tall, handsome young man in his early twenties, dressed in the glorious uniform of the FFI (Forces Françaises de l'Intérieur), the French army that has reconstituted itself in the last few months. He is wearing a large, fancy beret. Medals are decorating his chest and a fancy braid hangs from his epaulet. He does look like a hero.

"Paul!" Maman and Papa exclaim at once. From the way they greet each other and address one another in the intimate tu, *I know it has to be someone special.*

He hugs and kisses my sisters and me, as our eyes beg for an explanation.

"Well, young lady, don't you remember me?" he asks, addressing me. "I fed you your very first bottle!"

Of course I don't remember, but I certainly wish I knew more about this newly found cousin, who, I now understand, is the oldest son of my mother's older sister, Dora.

I do know of Paul and his younger brothers, Albert and Henri, and Aunt Dora and Uncle Ferry. They, too, lived in Alsace before the war, but much further away from us than my Aunt Fanny, and we probably didn't get to see them as often. And when the Jews were expelled from Alsace, they fled to Moutiers in Savoy, where they stayed in hiding until the end of the war.

Paul is obviously happy to be with us. We have so much to catch up on!

I also know that a neighbor denounced them in Moutiers, and that his father was arrested and sent to the French internment camp of Rivesaltes, near Perpignan, where he died. But I need to hear about it.

"Do you know who denounced you?" *I ask, feeling the anger swell inside me.* "Why would people inform on other people? What was in it for them?" *I hear my voice rising.*

"I wish you wouldn't talk about those things, Renée!" *Maman interrupts.*

"That's all right, Marguerite. Let her ask. She has a right to know," *says Papa.*

"No, Renée. We never found out who denounced us," *Paul says.* "You know," *he reflects, fidgeting with his beret,* "I've asked myself the question many, many times. I've discussed it with friends, too. What kind of person would denounce a Jew? Anyone who was envious of his apartment, his business, his life-style—real or imagined—or someone who had always disliked Jews and now had a chance to act on it. . . . It was not a very pretty picture, I'm afraid! At least I didn't have to sit and take it! I've been able to fight my own war!"

He explains with obvious pride how he joined the maquis—

the underground—as soon as he was of age and fought the milice—the despicable French military units that enforced the German rules during the Occupation and countered the French resistance.

As he is speaking, I wonder about his father, my Uncle Ferry. I don't really remember him. I wish I had known more about him—as about my mother's brothers from Hungary, who perished in Auschwitz—so that I could at least hold on to some memories.

"At least we can breathe again and resume a more normal life," Paul is saying. "My mother and my brothers will be returning to Strasbourg, but I still have work to do: The Germans have been pushed out of Paris, but they haven't surrendered yet!"

In the several weeks Paul is stationed in Paris, he opens a whole wide world to us, a world we were cut off from while in hiding. He tells us about the resistance and the underground—groups of men and women who sprang up all over the country because they refused to go along with the French government, which so shamelessly collaborated with the Germans.

"Imagine," Paul explains, "the chief of the French state, Marshal Pétain himself, encouraged our young men to go to Germany to work for the enemy! Young boys from eighteen up were picked up everywhere and forced to go!" As a result, I learn, more and more people joined the resistance and went into hiding.

"I got to meet some wonderful people," Paul often says. "People who took on code names to outwit the enemy, people who refused to talk under the cruelest of tortures. Of course, all this couldn't have happened without the help of the people in the small towns and villages who let us stay overnight or brought us food on the sly."

"Did you ever get into trouble?" my father asks him once.

"Twice!" Paul admits. "Oh! We were always in danger of being caught. I was lucky. Some of us did get caught and were sent to concentration camps, just like the Jews."

Paul also tells us—unofficially—that in France, one Jew out of four was deported. Does that mean that three out of four were saved by the French, one way or another?

My favorite moments are when, to raise our spirits, we all put our heads together and name all the great people and thinkers who have been Jewish.

"We need to take pride in our being Jewish!" Maman invariably concludes.

I listen and smile and feel my best. But I feel worried and alone the moment I leave our apartment.

Once the excitement of the arrival of the Allies wore off, people in Paris, like those in the rest of the country, returned to their daily lives—with one difference: Now they could air their long-held-in grudges. One remark would lead to another, and accusations would bounce wildly from person to person.

"How dare you get out the French flag after you've so openly admired the boches?" one storekeeper would ask another.

"I don't have to answer you, do I?" the other would snap back. "At least I didn't inform on my Jewish neighbors, the way some people did!"

It was showdown time and I, too, settled my accounts in my own way: When we returned to Paris, restrictions against the Jews had been lifted and Mme Durand, the owner of the dairy store my family was assigned to use during the war, was all peaches and cream to us. But I remembered how she had treated us, and refused to greet her. The witch had no business refusing to sell milk to my mother a couple of minutes after four—at that time Jews were allowed to shop only between three and four—after she'd had to wait in line at the grocery store and the *charcuterie! "You've got to get yourself better organized, Madame Roth!" she'd had the nerve to say.*

And when the food rationing ended, I stopped going to her store altogether.

Some appalling events took place in Paris during the weeks following the liberation: Women who were known to have gone out with German officers were dragged out in public, their hair shaved. Some onlookers spit at them or screamed insults. I ran past them or looked away whenever they were shown in the newsreels at the movies. I couldn't watch those poor wretches being so humiliated. Why didn't people leave them alone? I thought. They certainly did the least harm of all and only hurt themselves! It was as if people needed someone new to turn their scorn on now that the Germans—and the Jews—were out of the picture.

Much more shocking was the fact that when the Germans fled, some of the fiercest French collaborators felt so lost that they followed them to Germany! And that Marshal Pétain and other French officials were exiled or tried and found guilty of betraying their country. At least some justice was being done!

Fortunately, I conclude as I shut my eyes to go to sleep, Murray doesn't have to go to war and be a hero. But everybody says that the military inevitably turns a boy into a man.

Let's hope that will be the case for Murray.

Saturday, May 19

Rita and I are on our way home from the supermarket. It's hard to believe that Adele has been gone for one week—and that I have survived! One morning, she announced point-blank that it was time for her to take a trip—a combined business and pleasure trip, she called it. She was planning to go to Israel and then to Milan and Paris to get a new supply of leather items—gloves, belts, handbags—to resell to friends and acquaintances.

"I just do it for the fun of it!" she had explained once when in Paris. "It pays for my trip, and my friends are delighted to get a purse or a pair of gloves from Italy or a belt and a scarf from Paris."

Just my luck! I have hardly had enough time to get adjusted to this new world, and off she goes, leaving me with the awesome responsibility of taking care of her daughter, her husband, and the household!

"How will I be able to manage all by myself?" I panicked.

"You will! Of course, you will! Rita is a big girl, and the two of you get along so well! I've worked it all out: You'll have Sundays off, and Giza would love to have you then. You'll also be paid twenty dollars a week for the extra effort. You'll see; I'll be back in no time!" Adele added, putting on her famous smile and her velvet voice.

Now she is paying me, when she should have done that all along!

Actually we have *all* survived very nicely. Rita is allowed to spend more time at Sally's, and I am enjoying not having anyone on my back. Stanley doesn't say much, except that perhaps this may be the time for me to contact Molly and Irving Singer, whose greetings Adele brought us when she first visited us in Paris. I had nearly forgotten about Irving and Bernard Singer, Uncle Maurice's two older brothers, who emigrated to this country directly from Hungary years ago. But there must be some good reason why my mother—the most faithful, reliable letter writer who ever existed, who's kept a steady correspondence with everyone she ever knew, even if she hasn't seen them in years—didn't have them on her list!

=======

Rita is definitely preparing me for motherhood. It's incredible what holding her little hand in mine does for me: It forces me to walk straight and to think things through in a jiffy.

"Why don't you stay in America for good?" Rita asks. "Even *you* admit that life is easier here!"

She enjoys coming up with questions like that at the worst possible times—like now on Saturday morning when I am worried about planning tonight's dinner.

"I do admit that. But, remember, France is still recovering from a devastating war. Things will ease up in time. And just because life is easier here doesn't mean that everyone wants to move to America! People are very attached to their family and friends, their home, their land, their language, their customs. And they are used to a certain way of life. It's very difficult to leave all that behind!"

"It would be nice if you did move here, though. That way I wouldn't have to say good-bye to you!" Rita says, turning her face to me.

"That's very sweet, but I *must* return. Paris is where my family and my boyfriend are. But then, you never know, I may come back some day!"

I am amazed at what I have just said. The possibility has never occurred to me before. Am I finding a second home here, after all?

=======

Adele is certainly grooming me to be a *balabusta*—a homemaker—my mother's ideal of what a girl should be, but definitely not mine—I tell myself when, later in the afternoon, I am preparing dinner.

Rita, who is reluctantly setting the table, asks, "Renée, tell me honestly: Do you *really* like to cook and clean? You're always singing when you do!"

At least she doesn't burden me with leading questions about her future. One day Rita wants to be a ballerina. The next day she swears she's going to be a teacher. Another day, yet, she dreams of being a nurse. It must be mind-boggling to have to settle for one possibility when you have so many choices available!

Let's see, I think to myself. How can I be honest? I can't stand household chores. They are a waste of precious time that could be used much more creatively.

"Actually," I say, "I *do* like to cook, but I'm not crazy about cleaning pots and pans, about peeling potatoes and carrots, or about tidying up the house. Between you and me, I don't know anyone who is. It's just one of those things that people *have* to do, whether they like it or not. I happen to find that singing makes it less boring. Besides, there's something satisfying about a home that's spic and span, where everything is in its place. And somebody's got to do it!"

Is it possible that it's *me* saying that? As soon as I am away from Maman's nagging, I become her spokeswoman!

"I guess so," Rita replies. "But boys are not expected to do all those things. It's not fair!"

You can say that again! I echo silently. But this is not the time to get into a boy-girl comparison. God knows I have my own list of grievances in this area!

"Look, Rita," I say instead, suddenly in a more serious mood. "All I can say is that during the war, I was so homesick and so afraid that I would never see home again that I swore I would never, ever complain about chores! I guess I'm just plain grateful to be here, alive, and to be able to peel, clean, and cook!"

I detect a welcome sizzling sound in the oven.

"Just a minute, Rita. Let me check the bird!"

I am waiting for the chicken to brown and soften under the orange sauce. I've never had chicken à l'orange before. At home, chicken was a luxury, and when we had it, it was usually chicken paprika. I came across this recipe in one of Adele's magazines. It looked appealing and fairly easy.

Rita is standing at my side as I poke the bird. It is as tough as it was when I put it into the oven a good hour ago. There's *got* to be something wrong here.

I raise the temperature and squeeze some more juice onto the bird. I'll give it another few minutes.

Stanley is in the living room, enjoying his newspaper. He's been very helpful, asking me what I need, providing ample money, and showing interest in Rita's every activity. Actually, he's more relaxed than I have ever known him to be.

"It smells delicious!" he remarks now, encouraging.

"Do you know anything about chickens?" I finally ask him. "This one doesn't seem to get baked. It's over an hour now!"

"Sorry; I'm not much of a cook! Why don't you call Giza or Judy?"

I opt for Giza. I explain as best as I can on the phone that the longer I roast my chicken, the tougher it seems to get. I don't understand it: I bought it at the supermarket this very morning. It was marked *fowl,* which, as far as I know, is the same as poultry.

"Not quite," Giza explains, laughing. "*Fowl,* here, refers to an old hen, usually used for soups. It has to be cooked—simmered—for hours!"

I am mortified. Thank heavens, my mother and Adele are miles away!

"You learn best through your mistakes!" Stanley roars, slapping his thigh.

He's such a good sport! He could've been mad.

"Come on, girls, I'll treat you to a pizza!" he decides.

I don't dare make a face. Pizza is not my idea of a treat.

Thursday, May 24

Since Adele left, Rita has been following me around. I let her. She has only heard from Adele once, and I know she misses her.

Rita also insists on showing me every piece of homework. I go over her math, checking her fractions and divisions. But now she wants me to do more. "Could you read my report?" she asked me yesterday, handing me a couple of pages due for her American history course. It was titled "The Louisiana Purchase." I read it to check the spelling first—I am an excellent speller—but then I became quite interested in what I was reading because of its French connection. Louisiana had first been colonized by the French and was named after our King Louis XIV. The whole subject of the early settlers and the pioneer spirit is just fascinating to me. It must have been an exciting period!

While I am getting acquainted with the makings of America, Rita is getting a glimpse of Europe. Actually, she has a new *marotte*—favorite pastime—which I have passed on to her: geography.

We've adopted the globe on Murray's desk. It puts the whole world at our fingertips at a single glance. We put a marker to follow Adele's trip, based on the postcards we receive. It is incredible that France is such a tiny area and that Paris and Mulhouse, my hometown, are just dots, when they mean the world to me. I wanted to show Rita where Flers was—it wasn't even on the map!

I'm also following very closely the goings on in the building. The tenants are in an uproar: There has been no hot water in three days.

"I haven't been able to take my bath in three days," Rita whines.

I smile. What's the big deal? I always want to say when people get themselves all worked up about something unimportant.

"What are you smiling about?" Rita wants to know.

"I smile because you all take so much for granted. You turn a faucet, and out comes this wonderfully hot, steaming water. And then you have a wonderful bathroom where you can take as many baths as you want!

"What would you say if you *always* had to warm up or boil water on the stove for everything—as many still do in Paris? Or, as we did for three solid months in the barn after the landing of the Allies, how would you feel if you had to make do with ice-cold water from a stubborn pump—with no soap and no towel to dry yourself off?"

I could go on and on, but I certainly don't want to sound preachy.

"Actually," I continue, "there is a good thing to be said for the war restrictions and deprivations: They forced people to devise all sorts of ingenious tricks. I remember how I looked forward to reading in the newspapers about advice from this person or that one, such as using scutch grass to make the water sudsier or lining clothing and shoes with newspapers to keep warm."

"Wow! It must have been awfully cold to get to that!" Rita commented.

"People also develop a sense of humor and a new sense of what's important and what isn't."

"Do you think we should warm up water to fill the bathtub?" Rita asks.

"We could do that, although it's likely to take all evening to fill it up. But it's up to you."

"I think I'll stick to the bathroom sink tonight!" Rita concludes.

=====

The tenants are preparing a petition now. Stanley says that they are talking about withholding the rent money until all repairs are done. It is not just the hot water—there have been other complaints, and the tenants are just fed up.

I must give them credit. People here seem to know how to organize themselves. But more important, I think, is that people here feel they have rights, that they are entitled to certain givens, and they fight for them.

I wish tenants could get together in Paris, too. We had our share of problems. For weeks, it rained in our living room. We live on the top floor and had to eat holding umbrellas over our heads. Our landlord, M. Deschamps, just wouldn't fix the leaks in the roof.

So when it came to the roaches that suddenly invaded us, we didn't trust M. Deschamps to do anything without encouragement. Oh, he was always a gentleman, tipping his hat whenever he met us, or smiling at us from his seat in the neighborhood movies on Wednesday nights. But that was no longer enough. Our next door neighbor, Mme Chavignat, who always had a way to deal with problems, came up with a brilliant idea: She caught a few roaches, sealed them in an envelope, and put it under the door of his apartment. It didn't take him very long to get us the exterminator!

Saturday, May 26

Catching Sid Caesar in "Your Show of Shows" remains one of the highlights of my weekends. He is particularly funny tonight. He is portraying a lady waking up in the morning and getting ready for the day. He mimics putting lipstick on, and he is hilarious as he smears the lipstick all the way to his nostrils and draws an eyebrow pencil down and around the ears. He is *outrageous* when he portrays her zipping up her skirt: first one side, then the other, then the back—the skirt seems to be nothing but a network of zippers, some going up and down, some cutting across, others forming endless loops.

He always starts with an ordinary, simple gesture, something everyone understands and then, before you know it, the thing escalates until it becomes absurd. I am going to miss him when I return to Paris!

Sunday, May 27

Spending Sunday afternoons with Giza, Simon, and Joseph Rosen is another highlight of the weekend. It's a long ride to the Bronx, but I'm getting used to the New York subway. I always make sure I take a book along to distract myself from the reckless speeding, but I haven't read yet: I prefer to watch what goes on around me. The passengers do not, as in the Paris métro, sit quietly and offer their seats to pregnant women or the elderly. I cringe whenever a mother offers a seat to her child while she *stands*. How can children learn to be considerate of their elders if their parents spoil them so?

The Rosens live close to the subway in a large apartment complex. There are eight buildings—square, dull redbrick constructions, with no shutters, no balconies, no room for flower beds. All eight buildings look exactly alike from the outside—and inside, too. If I didn't count—go past two buildings to the left, then three to the right—I'd get lost.

From the moment I ring the bell, I am pampered: I'm not allowed to hang up my own jacket or help set the table or wash the dishes. Oddly enough, this may well be the only time in my life when I would *want* to help. Giza is not the most organized or fussiest homemaker in the world, and I must often restrain myself from clearing the soiled dishes from the table or wiping away the crumbs. I can't help smiling to myself: How angry I would be when my mother swiftly removed soiled dishes and plates. "Don't rush us!" I would yell. "We have all evening!" And now, I have become *her*.

But best of all, there is Joseph. At seventeen, he is lanky and not yet attractive, being still, as we say in French, in the *âge ingrat*. But he has the kindest, sunniest smile and the best of dispositions.

"A boy of seventeen should not be spending every Sunday afternoon at home," Giza worries week after week.

97

"Don't you worry about me!" Joseph retorts. "I have Billy to play chess with and I'm doing okay in school. I just like being home, that's all!"

I for one am not complaining: He is the attentive, adoring little brother I never had!

We always seem to drift into serious conversations as we linger at the table after lunch—mostly about Jewish life. It is that much more interesting because they are not, as far as I can tell, very observant. If I didn't know better, I would swear that Giza is eager to get me back into the fold. I wonder privately what the topic will be today.

"We've been thinking of rejoining our temple, from which we have drifted away in the past four years—since Joseph's bar mitzvah," Giza announces. "Have you been going to Jewish services in Paris?" she asks me.

"On occasions," I say, "for Kol Nidre, on Yom Kippur, to pray for my father. I'm not really comfortable in a synagogue." I hear my voice rising as I continue. "Going there reminds me of how women are simply ignored, kept away from the men."

I can't believe that it's *me* who is talking so openly about a subject that, at home, was never discussed and no one wanted to hear about.

"It's not quite *that* simple!" Giza protests. "Women *do* play an important role in the home. Don't forget, we are the ones who run the home and raise the children!"

I envy Giza's solid sense of Jewishness, which seems to have never wavered, even during the darkest days of the war.

"I'll find you some passages in the Scriptures that praise women," she promises.

I'm not about to give in so easily. "Jews all want boys

rather than girls! You can't deny that!" I say, not liking the challenge in my voice.

Giza shakes her head.

But I don't give her a chance to answer. I am carried away by a feeling I can no longer contain. "You tell me, then! Why did my father lie when my little sister, his third daughter, was born and tell everyone that she was a boy?" That question has been preying on my mind for many years.

Giza swallows hard. Obviously, she didn't expect such a question.

"It's rather clear to me," Simon replies simply. "Your father just wanted to have a boy to carry on his name, that's all."

I am stunned. That possibility had never occurred to me! Still, I do think that Papa didn't have to go *that* far!

"Well, I'm glad to say that things have changed," Giza points out. "In this country, there are plenty of synagogues where men and women sit together and pray together. If you want, I'll take you to one!"

"Sometime," I agree, not feeling up to it yet.

"Let's plan to go to the services for Rosh Hashanah!" Joseph suggests. "Please, Renée, promise you'll come with us!"

"It's fine with me. Just as long as I don't have to go to the second floor!" I reply.

III

SUMMER

SUMMER 1951

Saturday, June 9

Hurrah! My social life is expanding! I am on my way to
Evelyn's birthday party.

I've never been to a birthday party—mine or anyone's.
In France, people don't fuss about birthdays.

Murray had hoped that Evelyn and I would become
friends. So she called me in person to invite me. It would
be a nice way for us to meet—and for me to get away, she
pointed out. I shouldn't worry about going home late:
They have arranged for me to sleep over.

It is very thoughtful of her, considering that we have
never met. I wonder just how much Murray has told her
about me. I am dying to meet this mysterious person.

She gave me directions. I am to take the subway and get off at Atlantic Avenue in Brooklyn. There are only a couple of blocks until Stone Avenue, where she lives with her parents.

I am a bit apprehensive. I'll be traveling alone in Brooklyn, and I won't know a soul at the party.

Rita is excited for me. My hair is shiny and bouncy: She insisted on giving me an egg shampoo and a home hair set. She also helped me to select the clothes from my limited wardrobe: My pleated white skirt and the royal-blue blouse will do.

I leave at about six o'clock. It should take about an hour to get there, Evelyn said.

"Have a good time!" Stanley yells as the elevator doors close.

I walk quickly to the Astor Place subway station, the stop nearest us. After securing a seat next to the door so that I can dash out when the time comes, and frantically watching every station whipping by, I get to the Atlantic Avenue station—an important stop, judging from the many tracks and the many passengers who get off.

"Stone Avenue, please?" I ask the bearded face counting his money in the token booth, to make extra sure.

"There's no Stone Avenue around here, lady!" he informs me, without ever raising his eyes.

There *has* to be, if Evelyn said there was, I reason, and dash out to the street.

Block after block goes by as I pass clusters of buildings, grocery stores and drugstores, service stations with little flags shuddering in the breeze. It is endless. I have the feeling that I am getting nowhere and I am losing all sense of time. Why aren't there any old-fashioned gendarmes at the major intersections, as in Paris, to guide those poor lost souls who can't find their way?

Stone Avenue, near Pitkin Avenue, finally. The street is dark. I grope for number 70. It is a private house. The windows are brightly lit; laughter streams out. I have reached paradise. The door is ajar. Are they still waiting for me after two hours or more?

I push the door and make my way through an Italian-speaking crowd milling from the kitchen to the dining room, helping themselves from platters and platters of food. I'm trying to spot Evelyn. Hopefully, first she will spot *me!*

There is a young woman with dark hair, wearing a bright red dress, who is chatting with someone at the far end of the room. She turns her head. Our eyes meet. Our minds click.

"Evelyn?"

She rushes toward me. "Renée! You're here! I was so very worried!"

"Sorry . . . I got lost!"

She hugs me and kisses me like a long-lost friend. "I forgot to tell you to change lines and take the A train! I phoned Stanley as soon as I realized it, but you had already left! Come," she says, taking me by the hand. "Let me introduce you to everybody—starting with the food. You must be starved!"

———

Late at night, I am resting on my cot, squeezed between two strangers also sleeping on cots. I can't fall asleep because Evelyn's father is snoring so loudly in the adjoining room. I am tempted to whistle—my cousin Rolande assured me that it always did the trick with *her* father when he snored—but I don't dare, for fear of waking up the others.

So what if I can't sleep? I feel safe and welcome here, even if they are strangers, and I savor the feeling. Jews, Italians, what's the difference? We're one big family!

Sunday, June 10

"Renée! Renée!"

Someone is dragging me out of my sleep—which must only have come in the wee hours.

It is early morning. The sun is filtering through the blinds. Evelyn is at my side, her hair still undone, dressed in a blue terry robe. "Do you want to go to mass this morning?" she whispers.

I didn't expect the question. After all, I *am* Jewish, am I not, even though I was baptized? I'm really surprised that she knows that much about my past. Murray must have mentioned to her my hiding in Normandy. Still, I must give Evelyn credit for caring enough to think that I might, for old times' sake, want to go to church.

"Let's go to the kitchen," I whisper back. "Let's not wake anyone."

We tiptoe to the vast kitchen. The house is quiet. I wince at the bright sunlight streaming through the lace-curtained windows. The oiled red-and-white-checkered tablecloth shines on the large oak table. A basket is laid in its middle with a pile of country bread, waiting for hearty eaters.

"Do you go to mass on Sundays?" I ask.

"Sometimes." She confesses, "I'm not always a good girl!" She smiles.

"But isn't it a must? I mean, isn't it a mortal sin if you don't attend mass on Sundays and holy days?" I wonder. "Mind you," I add, smiling, "I'm not passing a judgment, just trying to set my memory straight!"

"You're right . . . I really have no excuses," she comments, visibly untroubled by the fact. I am impressed by her attitude—quiet and confident. She had evidently made peace with herself about it.

"I love to visit churches," I reflect. "Actually, it is strange how I always look for a church whenever I come to a new town—not to pray, but because it feels safe. But it just doesn't feel right going to a Catholic service since I don't believe in God anymore—especially since I never attend a Jewish service."

"I understand," Evelyn says thoughtfully. "You won't mind if I go, then, will you? My father and aunt will keep you company. My aunt can hardly get around—she has arthritis in her knee. As for my father, he never goes to mass. 'Church is for the women!' he says."

We take seats on either side of the table.

"I've been wanting to ask you something," I observe. "I hope you don't mind the question. . . . If you marry Murray, how are you going to bring up your children?"

She laughs her throaty laugh.

"Look, Renée. . . . The problem is not *how* we're going to bring up our children—I'm sure we'll be able to deal with it when the time comes. The problem is getting Adele to agree to the wedding. She's a tough one! Murray is now determined to get married with or *without* her blessing. . . . At least Stanley is on our side."

She is so totally trusting. It feels strange knowing something about Murray that she doesn't.

"Please don't think I'm prying. . . . You seem to have

such confidence in Murray, in your future together! He's going overseas and will be gone for many months. Don't you worry about it? I myself have a boyfriend in Paris and I have doubts about him sometimes, even though he writes to me almost daily."

"Look," Evelyn says, unruffled. "I don't expect men to be perfect. Besides, I realize that Murray is a bit nutty —but I love him. He makes me happy when I'm with him and he's very good to my folks. All I can say is that I'm willing to wait and hope for the best!"

She is certainly determined to get what she wants—and she wants Murray. I only hope that he will be deserving of her devotion. Somehow, I get the feeling that she will be able to take care of herself and to handle Murray— regardless.

"All right, then," I pursue. "Assuming that the two of you get married, how are you going to raise your children?"

"I haven't really thought about it. But it shouldn't be a problem, really. Murray is not religion-minded at all. I don't think he'd care one way or another. . . . And I don't, either."

"But your families might care! Murray doesn't have a large family, but Adele may still want the children to be raised as Jews. And you have a rather large family! Do you think your mother, father, and brothers will just say, 'Okay, do what you want'?"

"Frankly, it doesn't matter to me. I love Murray and all I want is for us to be married. For the rest, I'll do whatever he wants. . . . Maybe we'll raise them as both Catholic and Jewish and let them choose later!

"Hey! The coffee is brewed," Evelyn interrupts herself. "Let's have a cup, and then I've got to get ready."

Waiting for a child to be grown to choose between two religions? I ponder while savoring the strong coffee. No way! It's the *last* thing any parent should do! Children need something to hold on to—a set of firm, consistent beliefs to guide them along; otherwise they're fertile ground for anything that promises to fill the gap. Take me: If I'd had stronger religious convictions as a child, I wouldn't have been torn all these years and I wouldn't wonder, as I still do, where I belong!

Chances are that, knowing Fernand, our children will be raised as Jews—which is the way it should be. What if they pick up my love of churches and the Catholic hymns, though?

So what if they do? Actually, I rather *like* the idea!

"Got to go!" Evelyn reminds me, wiping her mouth with her napkin. "You're absolutely sure you won't join me?"

I'd certainly like to, but I just *can't*.

"Positive," I reply.

"I'll be sure to pray for you!" She smiles, rushing off.

Saturday, June 16

I am on my way to Broome Street, within reasonable walking distance from the Millers', to visit Irving and Molly Singer. I had finally taken the first step and telephoned them. They were not surprised to hear from me.

"Maurice wrote us that you were coming," Molly explained. "But we didn't know just when. I'm glad you called."

They live on the ground floor of a large apartment

building with well-tended grounds—a welcome green space in this very urban neighborhood.

I immediately recognize Irving. It's easy. The men on the Singer side have a marked family resemblance: the same strong nose, the same dark eyes and look. Irving simply has a slighter build than Uncle Maurice and has graying hair. He is the oldest.

He is also wearing a yarmulke.

He doesn't say much at first, just smiles and barely brushes the hand I extend to him. (I only learn later that observant men don't shake hands.)

It is Molly who does the honors. She must be American —she has no noticeable accent. An apron is wrapped around her tailored dress. She immediately invites me to the living room, where I am no longer surprised to find the coffee table, ruffled sofa, and assorted overstuffed armchairs that seem so popular in America. But here, they are protected by plastic slipcovers.

"We only use this room for company," Molly apologizes.

I discreetly look around. There is a brass menorah on the breakfront and a large framed picture on the wall of a bearded old gentleman teaching a young child—a *male* child, of course—to read from the Scriptures.

Irving has settled into one of the armchairs and observes me, sitting on the couch next to Molly. He immediately asks about his brother Maurice. When did I last see him? How are his sons? Are they religious? Even to my inexperienced ears, his English sounds heavily accented.

I am taken aback. Doesn't he care about how we survived the war, my father's death—not to mention my being alone in New York these past few months? "You must excuse my husband," says Molly, smiling forgivingly at Irving. "He's a religious man who spends a great deal of his free time in *shul*—synagogue. We have no children, so I have plenty of time to do volunteer work for the Hadassah and the O.R.T. That's how I met Adele."

"So, how do you like New York?" Irving questions.

"I like many things about New York," I reply.

Molly has prepared a little snack. There are slices of pound cake and a tea set on the coffee table, with a sugar bowl and lemon slices on a small plate.

"What can I offer you?" Molly asks.

"I'll have some tea. Thank you."

"You don't sweeten your tea?" she further inquires.

"Old war habits," I explain as I bite on a sugar cube. "One lump would last us for two or three cups."

"We keep a kosher home," continues my hostess. "Do you?"

"Not since the war . . . at least, not since we fled to Paris," I reply, determined more than ever to keep the inquiry to a minimum. There's no telling how they would react if they found out that my sisters and I have actually been baptized!

"Have you had a chance to talk to my brother Bernard yet?" Irving asks.

This man definitely has a one-track mind. All he is interested in is his family! Still, I am delighted to see him change the subject.

"No, not yet. Adele only had your telephone number."

"I'm sure he'd like to meet you. You know," Irving says with an unexpected twinkle in his eyes, leaning forward, "my brother used to see an awful lot of your mother back in Budapest. . . . She must have been eighteen, and he was twenty-one."

My ears perk up. I remember my mother at eighteen—from one of the snapshots that she keeps in a shoe box. That must have been after she recovered from the typhoid fever. She was thin and stunningly beautiful, with her fine features and her short wavy hair—much more attractive than my sisters or I could ever be.

Maman never kept from us the fact that Bernard took her to the movies once in a while. But then, they were second cousins. Nothing unusual.

Irving is leaning further forward, his crossed hands resting on his lap. He has suddenly become quite talkative. "You probably know, too, that Bernard promised your mother to bring her over to America—that was in 1925 or '26. But he never did. . . . Once you cross the ocean," Irving reflects, looking away, gazing thoughtfully at the sugar bowl, "you change. You get caught up in the business of adapting to a new country, a new language, different customs—and everything else takes a backseat."

Maybe he, too, is guilty of having let down a poor girl in Budapest? But I am hardly listening. I'm in shock. *My* mother coming to New York? This is the first time I have heard about it!

I have the feeling that I'm seeing my mother for the very first time—not looking at her as I always have, but seeing her as a surprisingly young and beautiful woman with dreams and wishes and vulnerabilities. How is it, I wonder, that I have seen only her overbearing ways? Why didn't she let us see the hurt and disappointed girl that hid behind them?

"There's no use going over the past. What's done is done," Molly remarks.

"I guess it was meant to be that way," I conclude.

But I look away so as not to betray my feelings. What kind of man is this Bernard, breaking such a promise to a young girl who may have even loved him? What kind of a *cousin* is he? I ask myself.

I bet Maman never even heard from him! No wonder she never talks about him! No wonder, too, that she doesn't trust Fernand to wait for me.

I'd love to see her face when she reads about my visit with Irving and Molly!

Sunday, June 24

I'm really dying to meet this Bernard to find out what he's like. He must be just as eager to see me, as he telephoned the day after my visit to his brother to invite me over. That's where I'm off to today. I had to give up my Sunday afternoon at Giza's, though; it was the only convenient time.

Bernard and his wife, Esther, live in the same apartment complex as Molly and Irving, but closer to the East River.

A middle-aged lady opens the door. She is frail, with an unsmiling, tired face, and is rather unstylish under her apron. I am jubilant. Bernard's wife—this creature he preferred to my mother—doesn't hold a candle to her!

"Hello, Renée! Welcome!" She says after I introduce myself. "Please come in. . . . I'm so sorry," she adds, in a small, whining voice, "today is a bad day for me. I have arthritis and it is acting up."

I instantly feel guilty for my uncharitable thoughts. Bernard joins us in the foyer. I notice immediately his strong nose, his dark eyes, his inordinately long eyelashes—like my Uncle Maurice. He has a full head of dark hair, surprising for his age—around fifty, I figure. But he doesn't wear a yarmulke.

He goes straight to the point. "So, you're Mancsi's eldest daughter!" he says after an energetic handshake. It is strange hearing him call Maman by her Hungarian name, which only close members of the family know.

"In person!" I say.

He examines me—my parents' handiwork—very closely. I *know* he is looking for a resemblance to my mother. He's wasting his time: I look like my father.

"Why don't we go to the living room? We'll be more comfortable," Bernard offers.

The living room is a carbon copy of Molly's and Irving's, without the plastic covers.

"So, do tell me . . . how's your mother? And your sisters?" Bernard asks. "Maurice wrote us that your father died. He was very fond of him. I'm sorry."

I explain as best as I can our life in Paris. He has so many questions!

"Excuse me for a moment, won't you?" Esther interrupts. "I'll get the snacks from the kitchen."

I'm grateful for the interruption.

"Fate plays strange tricks on us!" Bernard reflects. "I never got to see Paris, even though I had intended to go there. Somehow it never worked out." I think I detect a bit of sadness in his voice. Does that mean that he still carries the torch for my mother?

"You know," he continues, as Esther comes in carrying a tray with finger sandwiches and a teapot, "we had thought of inviting you for dinner on a Friday night, for the Sabbath. But it would have been much too late for you to go home alone. You see, we don't travel during the Sabbath."

"You *do* observe the Sabbath at home, I mean, in Paris, don't you?" Esther inquires. She has a marked accent, too—rolling her *r*'s—unmistakably Hungarian.

"No. At least not since we fled from Alsace. I have only vague memories about it from before the war."

"Your mother does *not* keep a kosher home?" Bernard exclaims.

The way he says it makes it sound totally sinful.

"Not since the war," I repeat. "We had other things to worry about!" The words are sterner than I meant. I wish they'd leave me alone instead of grilling me about my Jewish life!

"I hope you don't mind my questions," Bernard pursues in a more confidential tone of voice, leaning slightly forward. "I'm not as pious as my brother Irving, but I *do* think it is very important to continue the religious traditions, to observe the Holy Days—to be a better Jew for it!"

You, too? I rebel silently. Just being among Jews is good enough for me right now. Why does it have to be *practicing* Jews? None of the Jews we know in Paris are. And they don't consider themselves any less Jewish!

It's easy enough for you to pass judgment from the comfort of your living room! I'm tempted to tell Bernard and Esther.

"Look," I finally say, my feelings getting the better of me. "I may not be a practicing Jew, but don't you think that the hardships I experienced during the war *because* I was a Jew make me as good a Jew as anyone else?"

"I didn't mean it quite that way!" Bernard apologizes.

"Let the girl have some food!" Esther urges. "Here, Renée, have some of these." She hands me a plate with a couple of tiny sandwiches made of white bread.

"Thank you," I say, resting the plate on the coffee table. "Perhaps you don't realize that we are all still struggling to recover from these rather traumatic years," I explain, making a special effort to remain calm and collected—and not defensive. "You must understand: Papa's unexpected death—so soon after the end of the war—was not only a shock; our lives changed radically. You see, we were ready to move back to our former apartment in Mulhouse. We had our keys and the moving was set for January second, 1947, but Papa died two weeks before that. Maman refused to return to Alsace to join the rest of the family—there were too many painful memories—and so we stayed in Paris. And we never got to observe the Sabbath—I mean to light the candles or anything like that. Maybe because there was no man in the house? I'm not sure. But then, I'm not sure if we were ever *that* observant, anyway."

"You haven't touched any food!" Esther laments. The poor woman is doing her best to change the subject.

Actually, I'm much too agitated to eat or drink, but I force myself to take a bite from a hard-boiled-egg sandwich for her sake.

"It's quite good!" I comment politely, wondering what should come next.

I may as well tell it *all*! I decide. Why keep our conversion a secret?

"You see," I continue, hesitating, self-conscious about finding the proper words, "while my sisters and I were in hiding with nuns, we were baptized."

"*Baptized?*" Bernard gasps. "I had no idea!"

"The poor girls," Esther sighs.

"I assume your mother and father gave permission?" Bernard worries.

"Well, it was understood that the nuns would do what was best for our safety."

"But they may have been only too happy to convert you!" Bernard cries out.

"Except that they didn't convert us until the Germans came to our town almost a year and a half down the road. No, it wasn't the case, I'm sure!"

"And after the war, did you get a *tvila?*" Bernard pursues, relentless.

"A what?" I exclaim, wondering what he is talking about.

"A *tvila*—you know, the ritual that cleanses away baptism, or anything that may have tampered with the Jewish identity," Bernard explains.

"No. I didn't even know that such a thing existed! At any rate," I hasten to add, "it won't be necessary: I don't practice any religion at this point. I guess all I want is to be able to be a Jew in my own way, with no religious strings attached!" Is that so wrong? I think to myself.

"What a shame!" Bernard sighs. "But it's not too late!"

How disappointing! How disappointing that Bernard —and Esther and Irving—our *own* people, members of *our* family, yet!—have so little understanding of what happened to us. Maybe *no one* has. They are sadly missing the point. Isn't tolerance what it is all about? Why can't they just accept what we are—what we *can* be? The bottom line is that we are all alive!

So much for finding a friend in my mother's childhood sweetheart.

"I certainly hope you'll find a way to be Jewish again!" Bernard concludes, smiling.

"So do I," Esther echoes.

And so do I.

Friday, July 6

I knew Maman's response would be immediate.

"Did you look your best, Renée? What exactly did Bernard want to know about me? What is his wife like?" she writes.

I knew she would have loads of questions about my visit to Bernard's. Of course, I did not mention a word about his broken promise. She must have felt terribly hurt and betrayed at the time—and perhaps she hadn't wanted anyone to know about it. It feels strange, though, to be in on a secret about a parent. It is as if the picture I had of her—flat, in black and white—is slowly filling out and taking on some colors.

"Fernand came to visit last Sunday, and we asked him to stay for lunch," Maman further writes. The two of them are making an effort—finally! They didn't get on too well before I left. He bristled whenever she became overbearing. I'll never forget the day he slammed the door on her and left in a huff when she screamed at us for returning from the movies only minutes after my midnight curfew. Poor Fernand!

Sometimes I wish I could have slammed the door in Maman's face, too.

I bet *she* didn't have to ask for her mother's permission whenever her Bernard asked her out! I can't imagine Grand-mère being bossy. . . .

Grand-mère lived with us for as long as I could remember, until the family had to split up for safety during the war. She was quiet, never interfered with the goings-on at home, and seemed to be content just helping Maman with the peeling and the grating or holding tiny Lily on her lap when she was still a baby, her eyes looking aimlessly ahead of her because Grand-mère was blind.

She never made a fuss about not seeing. I remember that when the three of us girls were very young, we would ask her to play hide-and-seek with us. And she did. "Don't look, Grand-mère!" we would yell. We didn't realize then that she could never cheat.

Maman was always so attentive to her and catered to her every need, polishing her nails, tending to her face and hair, admiring her smooth skin. Even when Grand-mère became sick in later years and accused her of poisoning her food, Maman always forgave her and blamed it on her blindness.

Could someone explain to me why Maman—so loving and caring with her mother, her sister Fanny, even strangers—is so unfair and demanding of me?

How I wish now that I had known more about her life before us, about her father who died before I was born— and about Bernard!

Someday, Maman and I will have to sit down and catch up on things—on what dreams she had when she was a girl.

Sunday, July 15

The neighborhood church bells are pealing melodiously, echoing in the mild morning air as in my heart. The sound unfailingly brings me back to those Sundays in Normandy when my sisters and I, properly hatted and gloved and carrying our gold-rimmed missals, would rush to St. Jean, our parish church, accompanied by Sister Madeleine. Will I feel as strongly about church bells for the rest of my life?

As usual, I'm on my way to Giza's. After lunch, Joseph and I plan to visit the Bronx zoo. We're so lucky to have one in the area!

======

The zoo is only a bus ride from Giza's. We have entered the large park, already crowded with visitors. Joseph is perfectly happy to escort me to my favorite spot: the monkey cage. I rush through the crowd of parents and children, as I always did in the Mulhouse zoo or the one in Vincennes, near Paris, to get to the orangutans, the chimpanzees—all of them. I am a child again as I watch them in fascination, standing erect on their hind legs, peeling a banana or crushing a peanut shell between their teeth, frowning as if they were thinking—so close to us that I expect them at any moment to say, "Thank you," or "More, please!" whenever they stretch their hands to the onlookers.

======

Joseph and I are now walking through the park. It is quite warm and I have taken my shoes off, treading the soft grass. It feels wonderful. I smile at Joseph, this miraculous younger brother. I look longingly at a threesome wandering by—a mother tightly holding an infant in her arms while the father is pushing the stroller—and, further along, at a handful of teenagers sprawled out on the lawn, snapping their fingers to the beat of a tune streaming out of a nearby radio. This is the picture of a happy, carefree Sunday afternoon. I long to feel a part of it all, but this past I carry with me sets me apart. I am just a child looking through the fence at someone else's party.

I spot a bed of flowers emerging from the grass. Spontaneously, I pick one of them. I suddenly need to collect myself, to better see, touch, smell the flower, to experience this special moment. I block out the children's shrieking, the happy passersby. How delicate the white pistil, the yellow petals curving out, opening to the daylight and the sun. Frail and yet so strong! So beautiful, yet meant to live just a few days.

"If you're so taken by God's creatures, then you must believe in Him!" Giza remarked the other day.

I wish I *could!* I wish it were that simple.

But when I marvel at the sight of a flower, or delight in the sound of a cricket on a summer night, it is *life* that I am celebrating, the prodigy of still being alive. And deep within me I know that I am seeing, smelling, touching for Feigie, for Monique—and for all the countless other children whose lives were snatched away just because they were Jewish.

I can't think beyond that. I still can't bear the idea of their having been killed in Auschwitz. My mind simply shuts down. The only fleeting thought—the only prayer, perhaps—that I allow myself from time to time is the hope that they were with their parents to the end and that death came instantly.

How could God really exist and allow such a massacre? I may need a lifetime to think it through.

Still, in spite of myself, my hands join toward the sky as if in prayer, needing someone to whom I could say, Thank you for being alive. Thank you for this moment!

"What are you thinking about?" Joseph inquires, interrupting my reverie.

"It's very complicated," I reply, taking his arm affectionately, grateful for his presence. "Maybe we'll talk about it another time. Let's continue our walk."

But thoughts of the war linger—flashing, nagging, crashing on this peaceful summer afternoon. How I wish I had someone to discuss it all with—someone who *knows* and understands and would help me get some perspective—my sisters, Fernand, Pépée, or all four of them.

The park around me vanishes and I am again at the beaches of D day, which I visited on my trip to Normandy five years after the landing. Madeleine, a friend from the office, has invited me to her hometown near the coast. I have wanted to see, with my own eyes, la pointe du Hoc, a particularly rough spot around Omaha and Utah beaches, at the start of the fifty-odd-mile stretch where the Allied troops landed on the morning of June 6, 1944.

I have wanted to see, with my own eyes, that place where 180,000 men—Americans, British, and Canadians—attacked in a massive sweep that changed history.

Even under a bright afternoon sun, under a cloudless sky, the rough, barren cliffs look mean and murderous, all edges and blades. From the top of the cliffs, amid old bunkers and shell holes, I look down in awe. In the stillness of the air, with only the sound of the waves gently lapping the beaches, I picture the young men, dressed and armed for battle, running out in droves from the ships that brought them to shore, still fresh from their little towns and villages, with dreams in their eyes, determined to fight for the freedom of their fellow human beings and confident that they would win.

They did.

They climbed those cliffs on ropes, into the fire and shells from the Germans above. My God! I think. How could they make it to the top?

They did.

But there were many losses. The Americans alone suffered sixty-six hundred casualties in the first twenty-five hours.

I have to see the American cemetery in St. Laurent-sur-mer: a wide stretch of grass on the edge of the sea with rows and rows and rows of identical, pristine white crosses and, from time to time, Stars of David.

Here you don't rush in and out and think of what you're going to do next. Here I am spellbound by the utter silence. My eyes are riveted to those thousands of graves. I walk slowly. I want to get to know them. UNKNOWN, *the first one in the row reads. But the next one bears a name:* JOHN BENNETT—*from Oklahoma. Born in 1922. Died on June 6, 1944. Twenty-two years old. I try to picture him: blond, with freckles. He probably had his life all planned: He would marry, have children and watch them grow, and spend Sundays playing ball or watching a ball game on TV. That June morning, he got hit by an enemy bullet and, before he realized it, his life stopped.*

I look for a little stone to put on the grave, as Maman had us do when we visited Papa's grave. Flowers die and disappear, but a stone will last forever. There are none in the perfectly tended grass.

Thank you, I whisper silently. Without you, I might not be here today.

I can't leave the area without visiting the German cemetery in la Cambe, only a few miles away.

There is no ocean in sight here. Only grass and trees—a vast ground with thousands and thousands of simple square plaques with one, sometimes two, names on each. In the afternoon sun, black crosses cast dark shadows on the grass. It is mournful, but extraordinarily gripping and powerful.

Small wreaths of fresh flowers have been dropped here and there. The men who rest here also died for their country, I remind myself. I am glad someone remembers them.

As I walk slowly past, I think of the young German soldier at the farm where we once lived. We—the nuns and their charges—and a group of German soldiers lived side by side for some weeks. This soldier caught me waving my hanky at the Allied planes passing high in the sky. I thought for sure that my time had come, especially when he saw my face and might well have guessed from my curly black hair and my frightened look that I was Jewish. But he simply walked away.

I wonder what happened to him. He couldn't have been more than twenty years old.

I think I hear the joyful, haunting sound of a merry-go-round in the distance—always a wonderful reminder of the happier days of my childhood.

"You don't think I'm too old to go for a ride?" I ask Joseph, grateful for the opportunity and welcoming the interruption.

"Don't you know that merry-go-rounds are as much for grown-ups as for children?" Joseph smiled.

"Let's go, then! My treat!"

I'm on my way to Klein's department store, on Union Square, only a bus ride from Tompkins Square. It's nice to have some pocket money—now that I'm being paid—and not have to account to anybody. I'm on my way to get a summer skirt and sandals.

Who could have imagined that there would come a day when I would long for a place in the shade? We have hot spells in Paris, too, but there, at least, you can breathe. Here, as soon as you come out of an apartment building or store, the heavy, sticky heat surrounds you. The street life has changed as a result. After dusk, people socialize on the stoops, escaping the small, airless, cluttered apartments into the somewhat cooler evening air. The women are dressed in wide, sleeveless sundresses. The younger—and more daring—ones parade braless in loose tops, while the men walk around with their shirts hanging over their pants—anything that helps! People of all kinds are thrown together by a common enemy: the heat.

There is suddenly a feeling of neighborhood. People are actually friendlier. The grocer greeted me this morning with a "How are you this beautiful morning? Is it hot enough for you?"

I'm trying to take my mind off the oppressive heat by exploring the areas extending east and west, and I always make it a point to cross Tompkins Square Park on my way to the bus.

Tompkins Square is practically deserted. I watch a squirrel as it whips past me. It stops by a tree, looking resourceful and strong. Squirrels seem always to be fending for themselves, with no visible family around, relying solely on their instincts.

My mind wanders back to Normandy. I have ventured by myself away from the barn, against Mother Superior's orders, looking for some food—wild berries, anything that I can munch on.

The air is quiet for the moment, free from the noise of planes and military trucks. And suddenly I see it, resting on the grass by the ditch, a quivering mass of fur: a rabbit. The poor thing is frightened. I see that in its eyes, in the movement of the heart racing underneath the fur. I kneel down and begin to talk softly, gently, reassuringly, my hands behind my back. It is lame and can't move. A rabbit that cannot run! Should I pick it up and take it to the nuns—and scare it even more—or leave it to an uncertain fate?

Unable to decide, on the verge of tears because of my own helplessness, I wait by the ditch for a long, long time. By chance—by miracle, Mother Superior will say later—a patrolling gendarme drove by. I hand him the animal, saving both it and me from despair.

The squirrel has dropped from sight. Time to walk to the bus stop.

In Paris, I used to love riding the bus. From where we lived, we could get to the Étoile, the Opéra, the *jardins de Luxembourg*, and anywhere in between. I preferred to ride early in the morning, when the bright sun capped the city with a golden glow, or in the pink light of the approaching dusk. So what if the bus was delayed in traffic? Sitting by the window, I felt privileged to ride around the most beautiful city in the world.

Wednesday, August 8

Fernand is all excited. In his last letter, he announced that there is a chance his friends from the jazz club la Huchette will be playing with Lil Harding at the piano. And the nicest thing of all is that he has been asked to play the tuba with them! "Imagine, playing with Louis Armstrong's wife! These things only happen once in a lifetime!"

"Be on the lookout for the Apollo!" he keeps reminding me. He would be happy in New York!

It is somewhat reassuring to know that Fernand has such an all-consuming passion for Dixieland jazz. It keeps him busy and out of trouble—I mean, too involved to bother with other girls.

He is also quite busy with the fashion course at the Napolitano Institute. He enclosed a sample of his sketches. He definitely has a knack for capturing motion—a skirt that whirls, pleats that fan out.

Last, Fernand is giving me a detailed account of his frequent run-ins with his Aunt Ida. Now that I'm miles away, I'm able to see things that I've never noticed before. I'm struck by how critical he is of his aunt—she insists on knowing his whereabouts, he complains. Who can blame her? Didn't he run away to Palestine one morning without as much as leaving a note? And yet, he raves about his Uncle Max, an incorrigible gambler!

Sometimes, this worries me!

Fernand added a postscript to his letter, and the more I think about it, the more disturbing it gets: He is now inquiring about serving in the military near Paris so that we won't be apart. It slowly dawns on me that Fernand will be drafted next July—on his twentieth birthday, less than a year from now—and will be in the army for two solid years. What if he is stationed in Lyons, Marseilles, or Nantes? It may as well be China. We would never get to see each other—neither of us can afford to travel. This means, I figure, that if I am to stay here the two full years, as planned—that is until approximately another year and a half from now—we will be apart for a total of three and a half years.

It's absolutely unthinkable!

Saturday, August 18

After three long months, Adele has returned—at last!—carefree and full of anecdotes about this or that place, as if her being gone for so long were the most natural thing in the world!

"I missed you so!" she exclaims, fussing over me, and for a few minutes, my heart leaps with hope and I believe her. But then she quickly adds, a sheepish expression on her face, "I'm sorry, sweetie. . . . I didn't get a chance to see your mother and sisters. . . . You must believe me—I was so incredibly busy every single evening!"

So busy that she couldn't take a few moments in the seven days she spent in Paris to see my family when she was just a cab ride away? She can keep her "sweetie" to herself!

I realize that I am *still* trying to build Adele into someone she is not, and never will be.

Rita is unpacking the many gifts Adele has brought her—one from every town she visited.

Stanley certainly doesn't act like a husband who's missed his wife. No prolonged hugs; no lingering, tender looks. Back home, my parents weren't exactly lovey-dovey, and they certainly had their share of arguments—mostly about Papa's disappearing on Sunday afternoons to play cards with his cronies. But they kissed warmly when Papa left for work, and Maman would always emerge from the kitchen to welcome him home in the evening. And, on special occasions, Papa would whip out a bunch of flowers from behind his back and Maman would carry on as if they were the most beautiful carnations in the world.

All Stanley wants to hear about now is Murray—Adele visited him briefly in Nuremberg, where he is stationed. "How does he look? How does he sound?" he asks. "He's been writing frequently to Evelyn, you know. . . . I guess he must be lonely, being away from home and all. By the way, Evelyn has been calling while you were away. She even invited Renée to her birthday party!"

"I know! I know all about it," Adele sighs. "Murray told me. . . . He's also talking about becoming engaged," she adds, lowering her voice, obviously not thrilled at the prospect.

But *I* am! It means that, as far as Murray is concerned, I'm off the hook!

"Renée has been absolutely terrific!" Stanley continues, winking at me in an affectionate aside. "She ran the house and was simply wonderful to Rita!"

Dear Stanley! I think to myself. What other man would be just as happy with a slice of pizza or cold cuts as with a gourmet meal, and ask in all innocence: "This is delicious—tell me—what is it?"

"I always knew I could trust Renée!" Adele replies, smiling her irresistible smile. "I wasn't worried for a single moment. That's precisely why I didn't rush back!"

Rita is heartbreaking: following her mother around like a puppy, even to the bathroom, asking her countless questions. Poor child! She's missed her so, and Adele probably doesn't have the faintest clue!

Later in the evening, as we retire to Rita's room for our usual French hour, Rita asks me to read her passages from *Le Petit Prince*. She loves to hear, as indeed I do, about the little boy moving his chair forward on his small planet so that he may watch the sun setting again and again. And she loves to hear about his boundless love for his rose and his tiny star.

"I wish I were Mummy's little rose!" Rita whispers.

I know the feeling. I wrap my arms around her and hold her tight so that she won't see my eyes shining with unshed tears.

"But you are! . . . And your dad's, too!" I protest, wishing someone would tell me just that. "Look here: You're big and strong—and you really don't need to be watered and pampered every single day, do you?"

"Can I tell you a secret?" Rita confides, wrapping her arm around me.

"Absolutely!" I proclaim.

She whispers into my ear: "I like it best when you and Mummy are *both* here!"

What hurts most is to watch Rita pursuing her mother's elusive love and not noticing her father's quiet but unwavering attachment.

IV

AUTUMN

AUTUMN 1951

Saturday, September 8

The idea of Fernand leaving for the military in several months is haunting me now. I've made up my mind: I've got to return to Paris next spring.

Dollar signs are flashing in my mind: I'll have to reimburse the Millers for the trip over and buy the ticket for the trip back. We are talking about four hundred dollars or so just to start! Dear God, I despair, my case is hopeless! I'll never make it!

Meanwhile, I've got to let Maman know about my plans. So I sit down at Murray's desk and, with my best pen, and in my best French, I write to tell her how important it is for me to be home by next May.

Thursday, September 20

Giza, Simon, and Joseph kept their promise. So did I. And so here we are, on the eve of Rosh Hashanah, about to attend a Jewish service.

"It is a temple rather than a synagogue," Giza explains. "People who attend call themselves Reform Jews rather than Conservatives. The prayers are in English as well as in Hebrew. And of course, the women and the men sit together," she adds smiling.

I am not used to this modern, bright building with very large windows—stained glass windows—and white, cheerful walls. I can't help thinking of the synagogues from my distant past—dark, poorly lit, where the men whispered or chanted in sorrowful tones, and the women and the children were on an even darker second floor, neither seen nor heard.

Attractive is the word that comes to mind. And *cheerful*. So are the people—families, for the most part, greeting one another outside.

"Happy New Year!"

"Happy New Year, to you and your family!"

"Sam is quite a young man, now."

"This is Sandy. She just started college!"

There is nothing tentative or furtive about these perfectly groomed people in their holiday best who proudly carry their Jewishness in full view of the world.

We are walking in. It is a large, well-lit auditorium. The walls are sparsely decorated with cheerful, colorful wall hangings depicting religious scenes. Families sit together.

In some odd ways, it reminds me of a church—a positive feeling for me.

More people keep streaming in. I have never seen so many Jews in one place at one time. They greet one another, visibly rejoicing at meeting again to celebrate this event—as if celebrating the Jewish New Year was the most natural happening in the world. The rabbi welcomes the congregation, and the ceremony begins.

For the first time in my life, I no longer need to hush or hide. I want to reach out to Giza and Simon to my left and to Joseph to my right and to the people beyond and say, It's wonderful to be here; thanks for making this possible.

I may never be a conventional Jew, like the people gathered here today, and I may always have a soft spot for the Virgin Mary and St. Joseph. Nevertheless, as I settle into my seat, holding my chin high and smiling at Joseph at my side, I know I have finally come to a safe harbor.

Thursday, September 27

I'm holding the verdict, Maman's reply, in my hand. A numbing coldness is reaching my fingers, my toes, spreading all the way to my heart.

"You can't just pick up and go after what the Millers have done for you!" Maman writes. "You must stay the full two years, keep your part of the bargain. Otherwise Adele will be mad. Think of your sisters. Denise may want to go to America. It would be nice if Adele could sponsor her, too!"

"Bargain!" I exclaim, with tears in my heart. The cold I felt a few minutes ago gives way to a flashing angry heat. I'm the only one in this world who's keeping her bargain! Adele picks up and disappears for three long months, and now my own mother talks about bringing my sisters over, too. That was definitely *not* part of the deal! I came here to perfect my English. Period.

"Six months can't possibly make that much difference," she adds. "So what if Fernand is in the military by then? If"—there we go!—"you *really* love each other, that shouldn't be a problem!"

I read and reread the letter so many times that the words are soon empty of meaning. "Must! Must!" I keep hearing.

A weight is slowly crushing my chest. I gasp for air—just as I did in Flers on those days when despair took over. I must move, walk, do something. Above all, I must keep calm. I grab the grocery list prepared for me by Adele before she ran out of the house this morning. I lock the door, ride down the elevator. I turn down Avenue A, grateful for people brushing past me. I need to feel surrounded, even if it is by strangers. I nearly choke with tears at the sight of a father holding tight to his daughter's hand, his face brimming with love as he leans to listen to her.

I take refuge in a five-and-dime store, amid housewives searching for a zipper, a bunch of envelopes, nail polish. It is a place where I know I can linger.

Why me? Why does it have to be *me* who must pave the way for my sisters? They can come to America if they want, but why do I have to be responsible for them? I'm only two years older than Denise and three years older than Lily. I *hate* being the firstborn! Especially since Maman has spent years telling me what a scatterbrain I am and how much wiser my sisters are!

I often miss the simple ways of the convent. No matter what question I would bring to Sister Madeleine, she would find some logical way to explain it: "The main thing," she would say, "is to know in your heart of hearts that God will always give you enough strength to get through your hardships."

We have long since parted from the nuns. Sister Madeleine is far away, in a religious community somewhere in the north of France, near Lille, and we have lost touch with her. I have also lost my faith, and God, too, is gone from my life. And so is my other pillar, Papa. I'm without a safety net. It's time to grow a tougher shield. I've got to write Maman that it *will* make a difference to me if I am to stay here two years, that it is *my* life we are talking about. And who says that Adele would sponsor anyone without any strings attached?

Monday, October 1

There is a brown envelope addressed to me, a business envelope. The handwriting is not familiar, but the stamp is from France. A closer look clears up the mystery: It is from Guebwiller, in Alsace. It *has* to be from my Uncle Maurice.

It is the only letter I have ever received from him. I run to my room to read it in privacy.

"Mamele," he starts. I'm all choked up. No one has called me this—my uncle's nickname for me—in years. I read on. It's so much easier to listen when someone calls me Mamele.

"Your mother tells me you're being unreasonable and

that you want to return home prematurely," he says. "She asked me to write and tell you to stay the two full years, as planned. I hope you won't mind my writing or take the letter wrong. Your mother knows my affection for you and she thought it might help."

So now he is betraying me, too!

I feel a wild, loud pulsing against my temples. How dare she! I rage. How dare she use him to put more pressure on me! Is this the same mother who always warned us against strange people and strange ways? Is this the same mother who, only a few months ago, demanded that I be back at the last stroke of midnight from a date with a safe, loving young man, who now denies me the right to come home, the only place in the world I thought mine by right!

What does *she* know about being stranded, alone, in a foreign country? My mother never even *lived* alone!

I am not being asked to stay here forever; but the prospect of remaining here for so many more months when the only person who wants me and misses me—and has found me, a needle in a haystack—is in France, is simply unbearable.

What if our fears come true and we aren't able to see each other for over three years?

I'll become a nervous wreck. I'll probably die. I can already see the newspaper headlines: YOUNG, HOMESICK, FORLORN FRENCH GOVERNESS DIES OF ACHING HEART. MOTHER BLAMES HERSELF FOR THE REST OF HER LIFE.

It isn't fair. I pound and pound on my pillow until I'm totally spent. If Papa were here, this wouldn't happen. We wouldn't be poor. We would be back in Alsace, living a comfortable life, like the rest of our family. And I could go on with my life, without a fuss, like everyone else!

Sunday, October 7

The doom I carry around grows heavier every day. It's over a week now since I heard from Uncle Maurice. Adele wonders why I am so very quiet. I am waiting until everything is settled in my mind to talk to her about my plans.

Since that terrible letter, Maman has written only once—an "everything is fine" type of letter, like those she used to send during the war when we *couldn't* say anything for fear of the mail being censored. Not a word from my sisters, not even from Denise. Surely Maman must have discussed the matter with them! It is only too obvious to me, now: Fernand is the only one who cares about and misses me.

I feel abandoned. The small daily events I looked forward to—splashing under the hot shower, watching the toast turn brown, lingering in the food market, taking in the smells and sights of the street—no longer interest me. I do everything in a fog, in slow motion. In the afternoon, when I have a couple of hours to myself, I walk aimlessly to wherever my legs will take me, looking for human warmth: Woolworth, the post office, the local library.

But it is the movie theater that suits me best. I went to one last Sunday, when it opened at noontime. There were only a handful of people scattered around. There, I could escape and watch the people on the screen lead happy lives and make decisions without heart-wrenching guilt or sleepless nights. Soon I was sobbing, choking, wishing I could spend the rest of my life sitting there, in an empty row, praying—yes, praying!—that my life might become enjoyable and easy, too.

I'd rather be by myself and spend the afternoon at the

movies today, too. But Joseph called me. He reminded me that they were looking forward to having me to lunch, as usual. He must have sensed that something was wrong, since I didn't go last Sunday and didn't call until the last minute.

Giza is at the door after the first ring. "What happened?" she asks, a look of concern on her face. "We missed you last week!"

Joseph is right behind her, taking my jacket and my handbag.

Simon, quiet but smiling, pulls "my" chair away from the table and invites me to sit down. Lunch is ready.

But I can't talk or move. This kindness and attention is more than I can bear. I feel more abandoned than ever by my loved ones back home. "Giza prepared a wonderful ratatouille for you!" Simon points out. "Come, sit down."

I still can't move. Instead, I burst into tears. "I've got to go home—to Paris—before Fernand goes into the military. But Maman forbids me to," I blurt out.

Joseph brings me a box of tissues.

"Come now, come now!" Giza says, wrapping her arm around me. "No one can force you to stay if you don't want to! Your mother probably reasons that the longer you live here, the more fluent in English you will be."

"No, she actually ordered me to stay! She even had my uncle write me!" I am sobbing uncontrollably by now. I take a bunch of tissues from Joseph's hand. "I'll never be able to hold out!" I protest between sobs.

"Please don't cry, Renée!" Joseph begs.

"That's all right. Give it a good cry! You'll feel better afterward!" Giza promises.

I try a tentative smile—the crooked smile of the survivor.

140

"You're all very sweet. But my mother doesn't care how I feel," I continue, somewhat calmer, trying to catch my breath. "All she's interested in is making sure that I can bring my sisters over. That's *not* what I came for! She's so unfair!"

I pause to blow my nose. "All this wouldn't be happening if Papa were still here. We would've been better off, and I wouldn't have had to come to America to improve our lot. And even if I did, he would never let Maman force me to stay!

"It's all *my* fault!" I continue, shocked at the thought, hearing myself say it for the first time. "It's my fault Papa died! I didn't hurry enough to get the doctor!"

"Are you mad?" Giza yells now, grabbing my arm. "You get that thought out of your head this instant! Your father died of a heart attack. Come on, calm down, *ma petite*. I'm sure you did all you possibly could. No one can keep another person alive, no matter how much you love that person or how hard you try!"

I have stopped crying. A weight has been lifted from me. The whole world feels suddenly lighter. Did I really live these past five years believing somewhere within me that I was responsible for Papa's death, carrying the burden of his loss all the way to America?

I look at Joseph. He has tears in his eyes. He takes a step toward me and hugs me in silence.

Silenced, too, Simon takes me by the hand and leads me to "my" seat.

"Thanks," I say, letting out a deep sigh.

The lights are out and I am lying in bed, my head resting on my outstretched arms. I am staring at the ceiling in the dark, going over the events of this afternoon. For the first time, I am not running from my memories—those dark, unsettling thoughts that seemed best left untouched. They are emerging into full view. In all those years, we never talked at home about Papa's death. Yet, for a whole year, we were reminded of it daily: We wore black armbands, we didn't go to the movies. Worst of all for me, I couldn't touch the piano. I'll never forget how Mlle Père, our piano teacher, on her first visit when the year was up, broke the mourning when she sat and played, with much gusto, the "*Marche Turque*" of Mozart—oddly enough, one of Papa's favorites.

"Your father would want you to play, as he would want you to have this tea and cake right now!" she reminded me.

I now wish we *had* talked about the evening of Papa's death. For months afterward, I couldn't look at a picture of him. For months, I thought I saw him in the street or heard him cough in the distance.

With my eyes closed now, I see again the bedroom as I came in the door, flanked by Dr. Diamond and M. Chavignat, our neighbor. When I saw my father, lying on the bed where he and Maman had slept for the past eight years, I didn't call his name. I didn't cry. I only thought I wouldn't be able to go to school in the morning. How could I worry about such an unimportant thing? I wondered, horrified. Maman was on her knees, whimpering like a wounded animal, her hands over her face. I looked around the room. Everything was as before: The pills were next to the glass of water on the night table; the bottle of cologne, which Maman used to rub Papa's chest, was still open. I finally dared cast my eyes on Papa's face. His jaw was limp, his eyes shut. I had never experienced such intense stillness.

I wanted to comfort Maman, but I couldn't find any words.

I put my hands on her shoulders. She turned her face to me and began to sob.

"Oscar! Oscar! Don't leave me!" she implored in a voice that sent shivers down my spine. "Docteur! Docteur! Faites quelque chose!" ("Do something!") she begged, joining her hands, as Dr. Diamond, still in his coat and scarf, walked over to the bed to feel Papa's pulse, going through the motions for Maman's sake.

"I'm sorry, Madame Roth," he said. "I'm afraid it's all over."

Maman started to sob again. This time, her whole body was shaking. Her face was frightening in her grief, naked as I had never seen it before. I so wanted to tell her something soothing—I'm not sure what—but the words got stuck in my throat. I remained without a voice.

M. Chavignat, who had kept close to the door, walked over to my mother. Taking her hand, he said softly but firmly: "Come on now, Madame Roth. You must be reasonable. You've got to think of the children. Just sit down a few moments."

Maman settled into the chair our neighbor was offering.

"Oh, God! God in Heaven! What did I do to deserve this?" she cried whenever she looked at Papa.

I wanted to vanish. What's going to happen to us? I wondered. Papa was so strong. He always managed to turn things around.

Life resumed—but it had changed color forever.

Every day, the memory of Papa grew a little more dim, and the lump in my throat grew larger. I had to learn the meaning of never again once more.

Tears are now streaming down my cheeks in an even, steady flow coming from deep within me. For the first time, I allow myself to feel how much I've missed my father, how I have never forgiven myself for not having said good-bye. But he must have known that I was rushing out to save his life, didn't he?

Everything seems so much clearer now. I'm not being mean, or selfish, as Maman seems to imply, to want to return to Paris. I'm just trying to keep afloat, braving the breakers that are pulling me down. Maybe she and Uncle Maurice see in me more than I see in myself. I am not strong enough yet to be the person they want me to be.

It begins to dawn on me that I'm still running to my mother as the only safe place in the world, accepting her dictates as the only way to go. Yet I am also beginning to see her as a frustrated, life-worn woman who best expresses her love through cooking and knitting and making sure her children get what she was denied.

"A woman who had to give up those children and trust them to perfect strangers—nuns!—to insure their safety!" Giza has reminded me.

I can understand: America is where her last hope lies. She missed her chance once. She is not about to miss it again. It makes me sad to think that after her years of struggle, she has not come to a safe harbor.

"Maman," I mutter. What a strange word in an adult's voice.

But I have rights, too. It is *my* life that is at stake. The answer is *No*. No more sealing my lips and swallowing sharp words that may cause her grief. I feel stronger, as if my true self is finally emerging. And it is not only Maman, I realize; it is Adele, and Uncle Maurice, even Bernard and others here. All want me to be something I'm not. It is time to make my own decisions, to live my own life.

144

My mind is made up: I *will* return to Paris in time to see Fernand.

I pull the covers tightly around me. I close my eyes and, before slipping into a restful sleep, I say farewell to my childhood—a past that is finally over and done with.

Monday, October 29

I am growing new wings. My determination to return to Paris by May or June has given me new energy.

I can't possibly stay at the Millers'. For one thing, I just don't trust Adele anymore. Also, I'm beginning to realize that I don't have such a fair deal after all: I've met another governess, from England, at the supermarket. She is well paid, gets the weekend off—that is, Saturday afternoon through Sunday—*and* has one evening off during the week. And she has traveled with the family to Washington and Boston!

So I have decided to do something about my situation. I have a two o'clock appointment with Mme Morin, the manager of the Bilingual Employment Agency, on Nassau Street, in the heart of the Wall Street area. I'll try to get an office job.

It took all the courage I had to get the appointment. I saw the ad in the New York–based French newspaper *France-Amérique*—"your best bet if you want a job with French!" Giza assured me. I don't even know how I got enough courage to dial the number. But the minute I made contact with Mme Morin on the telephone, I heard her accent—pronouncing *agency, employment,* and *salary* with the French intonation—and I felt reassured.

I've got to leave soon if I want to be there promptly. "I've got to hurry! I've got to hurry!" I whisper to myself as I grab the belt from my closet and wrap it around my skirt. For the hundredth time, I glance at my watch. "I'll never make it!" I despair.

By now my heart is racing, my forehead covered with tiny beads of perspiration.

What I need is someone to reassure me, to say soothing words like, It's all right, Renée. You'll make it! There's nothing to worry about!

Sister Madeleine understood these feelings best.

"It's something leftover from the war," she explained once. "You try to reason, to talk to yourself. But your guts still react in the same way—as if it were a matter of life or death. It's fear—plain and simple. The same fear that grabbed you by the throat when the deadly bombs were falling all around us. Remember how we were told to run to our rooms in the middle of the air raid on D day to get a change of clothes and a blanket, and we thought we might not make it back to the shelter alive?

"It got to all of us, one way or another. Take poor Marinette. For days after the bombing, she would stick her fingers in her ears whenever she heard the rumble of an airplane and scream, 'Enough! Enough!' Even our Mother Superior was frightened. She just was nowhere to be found! One day we looked all over the house for her—in the cellar, even. We couldn't find her. She finally confessed afterward that she couldn't stand to remain cooped up when the shelling started. She dashed out to the orchard and ran and ran until she was out of breath, waiting for it to stop."

I had not known that Mother Superior was so scared. She was the one who had taken the three of us Jewish girls in—at the risk of her life—and thought nothing of getting onto her bicycle, day after day, to scour the neighboring farms for scraps of food. And later, when we were hiding in the barn, she was the one who took us across the fields to church on Sundays, regardless of the Germans scattered around and the Allies about to emerge at any moment. She was the one who got us through the ordeal.

I wonder if she, too, wherever she is today, still frets when she must hurry.

At last, here I am, trying to find my way from the subway, looking for Nassau Street. I glance in passing at the winding, narrow streets, with buildings so tall you've got to tilt your head way back to see the sky. The streets are crowded with people—business people with briefcases hurrying along, employees on their lunch breaks.

I make my way to 20 Nassau Street and push the revolving door. There are several banks of elevators. I spot one that indicates floors eighteen to thirty-five. The agency is on the thirty-fifth floor. I've never been on such a high floor in my life. The elevator is crowded. I enter it cautiously. I don't really belong here, I tell myself, glancing at these serious, confident faces. But they don't seem to pay attention any more to me than to one another. Everyone is in her or his own world. I am just as anonymous as the next person.

I'm the only one to get off at my floor. I land in a long corridor. Which way do I go? Right or left? I take a chance: left.

Room 3508. BILINGUAL EMPLOYMENT AGENCY it reads in gold letters on a wooden panel. I am impressed. I am on Wall Street, I remind myself, wishing Fernand and my sisters could see me!

A well-groomed young lady looks at me through a glass window. "May I help you?" she inquires. I notice her impeccable hairdo, her lily-white smile. She's pretty, and very sure of herself.

But I am not. I suddenly panic. I don't have to go through with this, I remind myself. All I have to do is go back to Adele's, and everything will return to normal.

"I have a two o'clock appointment with Madame Morin," I hear my voice announce. "My name is Renée Roth."

The receptionist looks at a pad in front of her.

"Please come in," she says. "Her office is the third door down this corridor. Just knock."

Mme Morin, it turns out, is a mild-mannered, pleasant woman, who has remained very French. She has no makeup on and wears braided *macarons* over her ears—a style very popular in France a few years ago, but which no one wears here. Her office is crowded with file cabinets and several typewriters sitting on movable tables. The wall behind her large desk is covered with framed diplomas and plaques.

She invites me to sit down and proceeds to tell me about her agency, a well-established firm that she has been running for the past twenty years. Twenty years and still speaking with such a marked accent? I wonder.

She asks me to fill out an application. "The fee is a month's salary," she explains. "It's standard procedure."

I agree to a shorthand test and a typing test in English. Even if I'm not to use all my skills right now, she wants to make sure my file reflects them.

My shorthand is good. I know it. I have difficulty with the typing, though.

"The French keyboard is different," I apologize.

"I know, I know. Don't worry about it," she assures me. "I can tell that your English is quite good."

I have passed, I know. Yet, I am waiting for the verdict with sweaty palms and a racing heart. If she offers me a job, I can't refuse it, can I?

She sits down at her desk, flips through a card file, and pulls one out.

"I do have a clerical position—mainly filing and light typing. A reading knowledge of French is required because of some French correspondence. You would be working for a commercial publication, the *American Exporter*. You may start on November fifteenth, if you're interested."

"And what's the salary?" I ask, clearing my throat, still not quite believing that it is *me* who is sitting here, about to take this gigantic step.

"Forty dollars a week to start. There will be an increase after three months, which is in essence a trial period."

I've got a job! I did it! I did it! I scream inside my head, wishing I could tell the whole world.

Instead, I summon all the poise I can to thank Mme Morin and to tell her that I am interested but that I need a couple of days to think things over.

"Call me on Monday if you want the job so that I can arrange for an interview," she says.

As soon as I close the door, I let out a yell. "I did it! *Vive l'Amérique!*"

There's no time to dawdle to admire the towering buildings. I've got so many things to do! I've got to get back by four o'clock to greet Rita from school and get dinner ready!

149

I can't get the key into the door quickly enough. Inside it feels warm and cozy. Hurriedly, I grab a hanger to put my coat on and throw myself onto the sofa, exhausted by the job-hunting experience.

I wish there were someone here to hug me, to tell me, "You're a brave girl. You're doing the right thing."

All I hear is the clock ticking away.

Unexpectedly, I burst into tears. Sorrow about leaving this cozy home, my first in America? Concern about where I am going to live after I leave here?

I don't feel so brave after all. I force myself to thank my lucky stars that friends like Giza will always be here to help me out.

I scramble to my feet: Rita is walking through the door!

=====

Poor Rita! I think to myself as I hug her a little later, a bit harder than usual, perhaps. I put on my apron and proceed to the kitchen to get dinner. Rita knows that her mother is not happy about the latest news: Murray's informal engagement to Evelyn. And she sees, too, the constant bickering that goes on between Adele and Stanley, mostly Adele's fault finding.

I wish Stanley would do something about Adele's constant criticism, something more than throwing his napkin onto the table and dashing out of the room.

"I wish there were something I could do to stop them from fighting," Rita sighs. "I can't stand it anymore!"

"I'm not sure that *anyone* can do anything. One thing I *can* tell you: It has *nothing* to do with you!"

As always, when Rita needs a lift, we end the evening by reading *Le Petit Prince*.

It always gives me a lift, too.

Tuesday, November 6

I know now that I will return home before Fernand goes into the army, and I have finally summoned up enough courage to write Maman about my plans.

Her reply is positively icy. My eyes brim with tears whenever I reread it. Yet, she adds a helpful postscript: "You know I don't approve of your moving out of the Millers' home. But if you do, be sure to contact Mr. and Mrs. Barth. Remember Clara and Alfred from rue François Miron? They live in New Brunswick, New Jersey, now, with their daughter. Not too far from New York, I understand. They may know someone in New York you could stay with."

Why couldn't she say, "Good luck" or "I'll write them a note myself"?

The Barths are no strangers to me. Both are childhood friends of my mother from Budapest, Hungary. They were the first people we knew in Paris. They welcomed all five of us to their small lodgings after we fled from Alsace in 1940.

They were not as fortunate as we were. They managed to hide here and there in Paris during the terrible years when the Jews were hunted down, but Violette, their eldest daughter, who was sickly and bedridden when we first met her, was caught and arrested. She died in prison from malnutrition and heart disease. She was not quite eighteen years old.

Whenever we went to the cemetery in Bagneux, near Paris, to visit Papa's and Grand-mère's graves, Maman always made sure we stopped at Violette's grave as well.

Eva, the Barth's youngest, married a G.I. shortly after the war and moved to America, and her parents followed.

I tell Giza all about the Barths on my visit today; and she insists that I telephone them right here and now. "It is Sunday. They should be at home."

I stand close by as she gets the number from the operator, my heart fluttering with anticipation as she finally dials.

"Here," she says, handing me the receiver.

"Renée? Mancsi's eldest daughter from Paris!" a voice exclaims. A string of undefinable but familiar Hungarian words ring in my ear. "You used to call me Claraneni, remember?" the voice continues.

Neni, I repeat mentally. The Hungarian word for *aunt* does come back to me.

Eva, the daughter, gets on the telephone, too. As a matter of fact, her parents *do* have friends living in the Bronx, the Schenkers—Hungarian friends—who also happen to have lived in France, where their son Jacques was born. They immigrated to the United States some four years ago. She gives me their phone number.

"But promise you'll come to visit us before you leave?"

I promise.

I can't help being amazed at the number of Jews who lived in France before moving to America. "Including you!" I remark to Giza. "France *must* have been good to the Jews then!"

"It was, for many years, especially in the twenties and the thirties. You realize that we'd all still be there if there had been no Hitler," Giza reflects pensively.

"But it *did* happen!" Simon says. "And, right now, *this* is the best country for us!"

While I have a phone handy, I try my luck with the Schenkers.

They are home. Mrs. Schenker answers. She speaks French with the familiar Hungarian accent, like my mother, rolling her *r*'s and leaving the *o*'s hanging in midair. She says that of course they would be delighted to have me stay with them. I could have my own room. And, since she cooks for just the two of them, cooking for three will make no difference. Actually, she adds, having conferred with her husband, not only would they be happy to welcome me, but she and her husband agree right there and then that they will charge me only fifteen dollars a week for room and board.

"How can you refuse?" Giza rejoices. "It's a wonderful deal!"

It *is* a wonderful deal. Still, I get the strange feeling that life is pulling me forward, and I am not quite ready to take the step.

Leave it to my mother, I think to myself afterward. She's kept alive all these years a very tight, worldwide network of relatives and friends that stretches from Brazil to Australia, where some of them have resettled after the war. A network that is solid, reliable—a *mespoche* (this is a Yiddish word for *family*) of a sort—for which the only password is to be Jewish.

Monday, November 12

I follow Adele from room to room, trying to find the right moment to tell her of my plans. Of course, there can be no *right* moment.

I finally tell her everything—right there, in the middle of the kitchen, where you can always reach out for the cookie jar or a drink of water for comfort—as she is putting away the dried dishes. I tell her about my wish to be back in Paris before Fernand joins the army, about my needing to raise some money.

She continues to pile up the dishes one by one on the counter, then abruptly stops.

"What are you talking about?" she says, letting go of the dishes and turning to me. "You mean, you *actually* found a job?" Her eyes register genuine shock. The rest of her remains as always: Her jet-black hair never betrays a gray root, her makeup is always fresh, her nails are always perfectly polished. "I'll be damned," she blurts out, letting herself plop onto the nearby banquette and playing with her large jade ring. "What are we going to do? What is *Rita* going to do?" she promptly corrects herself.

"Rita is a big girl. She'll be fine, just as she was before I moved in," I reassure her. I am surprisingly calm. My voice doesn't quake as I speak. "You know," she says, catching herself and smiling, "somehow I had hoped that you would like New York so much you'd never want to return. And that you'd take care of me in my old age."

I don't return her smile. "But you have your husband—and Murray and Rita! And I have my own mother and sisters to worry about. Of course, you know you can always count on me. But I have been here for close to a year now, and I think that, besides my need to earn some money, a change would be good for me."

"But how could you?" Adele suddenly explodes. "How could you just walk out, after all I've done for you!"

You owe me! You owe me! is all she has to say. It's all *everyone* has to say! When is someone going to admit that, maybe, they owe *me?*

"Look, Adele," I say, trying to hold on to the poise that is slowly slipping away. "You're not being fair, making me feel like a criminal. As I said, I'll always be grateful for what you've done, and you can always count on me!"

"What's going on?" Stanley inquires, coming in from the living room, where he was watching TV.

"Renée is talking about leaving us. She wants to work and make some money. Her boyfriend is going into the military in July, and she wants to be able to be home before then."

"She's found a job? More power to her!" Stanley says. "Actually, I expected this to happen sooner or later. She *should* get away from us. It's been wonderful having her here, especially for Rita. But while she's in New York, I can't blame her for wanting to get a better feel for the town!"

How I needed to hear this! "Thanks," I whisper.

"Still, she could stay with us, go to work, and pay *us* room and board!" Adele points out.

I have visions of working *and* being expected to carry on my responsibilities here. With someone else, I might reconsider. But not with Adele.

"I still don't think it's right to leave us, just like that. I had counted on another year, perhaps. After all I've done for you and your family!" Adele repeats.

"Come off it!" Stanley protests. "She's done an awful lot for us, too! You forget, you were gone for a good three months. We couldn't have done without her. You're not being fair!"

"Look, Renée," Adele finally says, with obvious effort. "I can't force you to stay. You're certainly allowed to do as you please. You're in this country legally, and you can be on your own, if that's what you want—as long as you're self-supporting!"

"What are you all talking about?" Rita has suddenly appeared, dressed for bed in her blue nightie and pink socks.

I walk over to her and take her hand. I want to be the one to break the news to her, rather than Adele.

"Sit down, Rita, next to me," I say, pointing to the banquette. "I've got to return to France earlier than I had expected and, because of that, I have to find a job and save some money. That means that I'll probably move out sooner."

"But why can't you stay until you leave?" Rita wants to know. I can't face her imploring eyes, so I look away.

"Because I couldn't possibly take care of you and the house and work full-time!" I explain. "You must believe me when I say that it has nothing to do with you. Anyway, I'll be in town, and we'll stay in touch, I promise."

"What's going to happen when Mummy goes away again? She said she might leave for a couple of weeks in March or April? Right, Mummy?"

"No one ever tells *me* anything!" Stanley protests. "When did that come up?"

"It's not a sure thing," Adele mutters. "There's no use getting upset about it *now*."

"Well it looks as if I'll be in New York at least until May. So I could always stay over, in a pinch. And I certainly intend to visit and go places with you. Maybe we can take that long walk across town we talked about!" I tell Rita.

"You promise?" Rita asks.

"Of course, I promise," I assure her, wrapping my arms around her.

Wednesday, November 14

I have been trying to get Rita to spend more time with her father before I leave, and my campaign is beginning to work. When the chips are down, it is always Stanley—not Adele—who is concerned about Rita's bruised knee or who checks her temperature when she has a cold. And I don't think Rita appreciates it.

"Daddy promised to take me ice-skating every Wednesday evening from now on!" Rita boasts as I am about to retire for the night.

That's precisely what I had hoped would happen after I encouraged tonight's outing. They both insisted on my going along—and I agreed, as a spectator only—to Rockefeller Center. The setting is so lovely. I never saw a skating rink in the open before, all lit up, and I just loved watching from the ramp above all those skaters, young and old, alone or holding hands, gliding on the ice in complicated loops and whirls.

Rita was graceful and moved about with a secure sense of balance. I didn't expect her father—stocky and overweight as he is—to be so fluid, but he took long, sure strides. He has always loved sports, he explained, and he used to take Murray skating when he was a youngster.

If it weren't for Stanley and Rita—who are both sad about my leaving but excited about my plans—life on Tompkins Square would be uncomfortable. Adele has talked me into staying another two weeks—even though I am to start my job next Monday!—and yet, she is icy in her attitude toward me. I can't quite seem to shake the heaviness that is settling on my chest. I don't want to get up in the morning to face Adele's reproachful silence. Her coldness is giving me doubts. Maybe I *am* an ingrate?

Maman is no help. She didn't even comment in her last letter about my getting the job—my first real job in America!—after all the anguish it caused me, which I described to her, blow by blow! She did say she was relieved that I had gotten in touch with the Barths in New Brunswick. She also mentioned having met Pépée and her mother, marketing in the rue de Clignancourt. "Really," she writes, "poor Mme Larmurier has gone *zinzin*"—slang for crazy—"not permitting her daughter to go out unless she goes along!"

The word sounds odd coming from Maman—she has always been such a stickler about no cursing and no slang. And besides, hasn't she kept a tight grip on me, too?

I am concerned about my friend Pépée. She sneaked out a letter to me again last week, stating that she couldn't stand it at home anymore. She is thinking either of running away to her cousins in Beaugency or marrying this very nice man who has been courting her for over a year and is so very kind to her—even if she is not sure she loves him. I can't write to her. Her mother intercepts every piece of mail she gets. So I wrote Denise to try to see Pépée and tell her not to make any rash decision, and certainly to talk her out of getting married. There must be some other solution, like moving out on her own. After all, she is working and she is over twenty-one.

Fernand is thrilled about my decision to return early. He drew up a special card to congratulate me on my new job—a clever drawing that links the Eiffel Tower and the New York skyline. He is counting the days, and is already planning to pick me up at the ship in le Havre and ride the boat train back to Paris with me. He needs to check with my mother, of course, just in case she intends to go all the way to le Havre to welcome me. He can't see both of them being there!

Neither can I.

I doubt if Maman would want to go. She's still mad at me!

Monday, November 19

How wonderful it feels to walk briskly in the cool morning air, along with the eager, freshly dressed crowd.

This is my third day. No more floundering about which way to go. I've come to "our" building on Fourth Avenue, and already it feels familiar. I walk to the bank of elevators marked 19 TO 35 and ride to the twenty-fifth floor. Our staff occupies the whole floor and is responsible for the publication of three commercial magazines serving an international readership.

My desk is one of six in what they refer to as the typing pool area. The various managers occupy small offices set all around the floor. These have windows that look out on neighborhood buildings. The more important people—the vice presidents—have more spacious corner offices, all carpeted and equipped with sleek, attractive furniture and decorated with colorful, modern paintings.

The view from our high floor is quite impressive. I'm a bit early this morning, so I walk to one of the corner windows to glance at the view: modern, angular office buildings and, in the distance, some apartment buildings with terraces and small gardens on the rooftops.

What a contrast with the small, quiet Paris office that I shared with three women and two men. It was located in a residential area. The rooms were small, looking out onto a courtyard. Everything was so very quiet that sometimes we could hear a pianist practicing Chopin preludes or nocturnes far away.

I walk over to my desk. I wish Maman could see it, complete with a hideaway typewriter, a movable chair, and a full set of drawers where I file the correspondence and the new subscribers' cards in alphabetical order by name and town. It's easy enough. Mr. McGibbons, my boss, told me—I'm still straining to understand his clipped British accent—that, in time, I'll be able to print the address plates myself on the addressograph machine.

He is so very pleasant! He finds something nice to say about almost everything I do. I hope he's not just being polite!

Maria walks in. She sits two desks away from me. She waves at me from across the room.

"Hi, Renée!" she says.

She walked up to me on the first day, even before we had a chance to be introduced formally. "I am Maria Sholton," she said, offering me her hand. "I overheard you speak. I knew you were French—or from somewhere in Europe. I am from Brazil. If you need anything, let me know."

I felt very grateful. She must have known how it felt to start a new job in a foreign country.

Maria is in her late twenties. She had been living in the United States for three years and is married to an American. She joined this office about a year ago and is doing what I have been hired to do, but in Spanish and in Portuguese.

Maria walks over to me. "We'll meet at coffee break, okay?" she reminds me.

"Sure!" I reply, eager for a new friend.

A young man waves at me from a distance. I wave back, but for the life of me I can't place him. How embarrassing!

On my first day, Mr. McGibbons—I'm glad he didn't insist on my addressing him by his first name!—took me around and introduced me to the rest of the staff:

"I'm Bill, from Editing."

"My name is Bill, from Accounts Receivable."

"Bob, from Engineering."

"Hi. I'm Chuck, the chief accountant. Glad to meet you."

Mr. McGibbons stands out, not only in the way he speaks, but also in the way he dresses. He is the only one who wears a white shirt with a starched collar and a smart tie folding into a vest. His pants are so well tailored and pressed that they make you forget how short he is.

The rest of the men are still only a blur of smiling faces. And the blur of faces belongs to a blur of names. I wish they were different, catchy names. Instead, they are all single syllables that sound interchangeable to me: Bob, Bill, Chuck. And when they take off their jackets and I am faced with a bunch of men who all wear white shirts, narrow ties, and bland pants, I'm totally lost.

I've been trying to make mental notes to help me tell

one from the other: Bill the accountant is balding; Bill the editor wears initialed shirts; he is not to be confused with heavyset Bob, the engineer, who likes to roll up his sleeves and is always munching on something, most often his pencil, or Chuck, who wears glasses and likes to show off his French.

If these were a bunch of Frenchmen that I had just recently met, their names and faces would most likely be etched forever in my memory. Why? I am trying to understand. It's not that Frenchmen are more handsome—they're not. Maybe it's because Bill, Bob, Chuck, and the other men in the office are all equally polite and say the expected niceties, but they feel so distant!

The coffee break comes around quickly. At ten-thirty sharp, a little bell can be heard by the elevators, signaling the arrival of the cart offering coffee, tea, and an assortment of rolls and cakes. What a wonderful idea! Maria and I are the first ones in line to get our coffee—served in paper cups—and together we walk over to the staff lounge, where we settle into a sofa. What an incredible luxury to have such a spacious room—equipped with sofas and armchairs as well as a small refrigerator and a cupboard for storage—where we can relax, have our coffee, or eat our lunch if we choose to.

The ladies' room next door is wonderful, too. It has a marble floor and marble sinks and hand towels and toilet paper galore. It even has a special area with a wall-to-wall mirror where you can sit down and check on your makeup. It won't be easy to go back to the humble ways of a Paris office, where my co-workers and I usually brought in our lunches in our tin *gamelles* and ate at our desks. But then, we had fun sharing our food in a potluck fashion.

Maria and I whisper to each other while the other girls come and go.

I admire their poise. I wish I could feel sure enough of myself to walk past other people in the room, sit down, and spend time in front of the mirror, and never worry about whether I should greet them first or wait for them to come to me. I wish I could not be concerned about doing the right thing and not care if people decide to ignore me altogether.

Maria certainly seems at ease. Like the others, she is perfectly groomed. I wonder if her long, polished nails, attractive hairstyle—cascades of auburn hair framing a lovely oval-shaped face and contrasting with her green eyes—and green eye shadow are part of her becoming an American?

Maria points to her watch: The fifteen minutes are over.

The afternoon goes fast. Mr. McGibbons shows me how to operate the addressograph machine. It's not hard at all, once you get used to the jolt to your body every time you hit that plate.

Now I really feel that I am doing something useful!

Saturday, November 24

Intervale Avenue, the Bronx. My soon-to-be new neighborhood.

Rita and I have just stepped out of the subway. Nothing has prepared me for this dismal street obscured by the elevated train and bordered on either side by equally dismal buildings. How can the poor souls in these apartments ever get used to subway riders staring into their windows, not to mention the racket of the passing trains?

Rita is just as eager to see my future quarters as I am, so we are both off to the Schenkers' where we have been invited this Saturday afternoon for *goûter* (the four o'clock snack customary in Paris). They live a couple of blocks away. The houses on the side streets are grayish and sad. There are not even any trees. I already miss Tompkins Square.

"Let's hurry!" I tell Rita, taking her hand.

I want to get the whole thing over with—Adele, the moving. I can't bear Adele's silences anymore. She makes it so hard to leave! When I offered to pay back the Millers what I owe them for the boat ticket from le Havre to New York just as soon as I am through with my debt to the employment agency, Stanley opposed it firmly. "No way!" he stormed, looking at Adele. "This poor child. It should never have been an issue!" But Adele remained silent. She didn't even say, "Sure, okay, let's forget about it!" It's her way of holding on to me.

We've come to a well-kept building with a stoop and a high, arched entrance. A narrow corridor leads us to the Schenkers' main floor apartment. There is no time to wonder: The minute the door opens, I am hugged, kissed, and fussed over—a little in French, but mostly in Hungarian. I am not only changing homes, I realize: I am switching worlds as well.

My future hosts are a lovely—if odd—couple. He, Willie, has an unusually youthful appearance: a full head of dark-brown hair over a pink, wrinkle-free complexion. She, Bertha, looks quite motherly with her very ample bosom, spindly legs, and grayish hair pulled to the back in a careless bun. However, her full face and a smile revealing two buck teeth give her an unexpected girlish quality.

They both speak French to me and English to Rita. As Mr. Schenker points out, they know enough English for them to get by—he as a presser, she as a buttonhole maker—in the garment district, where they both work.

"Why don't we show you your room before we settle down for *goûter?"* Mrs. Schenker suggests.

The apartment is "squeaky clean"—Rita's words. We glanced at the eat-in kitchen, not as spacious or as sunny as the Millers' but large enough to accommodate three people. I'm introduced to my room, spotless with its polished parquet floor and fresh curtains. It is of medium size and has in it all I need: a brass bed with a night table, a dresser, and a built-in closet. I'll be getting a small table and a chair, I am told, which I can use when I write letters.

"And now, time for *goûter!"* Mrs. Schenker announces.

We proceed to the dining room, which is separated from the living room by a glass door and furnished with a sizable oak table and six matching chairs. The china cups and saucers are already in place, and Mr. Schenker is bringing the coffeepot and milk on a tray. There are also filled pastries and other familiar Hungarian specialties.

"How very thoughtful, Mrs. Schenker!" I exclaim. "It reminds me of home!"

"Call me Berthaneni," Mrs. Schenker says.

We agree that next Saturday would be a good day for the move.

———

Rita and I are silent during the ride back, but I sense her need to snuggle up to me a little more than usual.

Dinner, too, is unusually silent, with only the sounds of the forks hitting plates and the glasses getting filled.

Adele doesn't ask any questions, so we don't talk.

"Rita told me you like your new place. I'm glad for you," Stanley says as he catches me on my way to Rita's room. "Don't worry about Adele. She'll get over it!"

How I need to hear that!

"And I'll help you move with the car," he promises.

Later, as I am tucking Rita in, she grabs me by the neck and whispers in my ear, "I have something to give you!" From under her pillow, she pulls out her dark-haired doll and hands it to me. "Your room at the Schenkers' seemed a bit empty to me," she continues. "So I thought that Melanie would keep you company. I know you like her best. You're always holding her!"

I am speechless. I never thought my feelings were that obvious!

"It's very sweet of you, Rita. Melanie *is* special to me. But she is yours!" I protest. "I can't possibly accept her!"

"I really want you to have her!" Rita insists, her nose crinkling happily.

"Thanks," I whisper, moved beyond words. "I'll take good care of her!"

V

WINTER

WINTER 1951–1952

Saturday, December 15

It's taking me forever to get settled in my new surroundings. It's over two weeks since I moved, and I'm still adjusting.

For someone who doesn't like changes, I've managed to be transplanted quite a bit in my lifetime, and this last time, it's been through my own choice! I miss Rita and Stanley more than I expected. Of course, Rita calls me practically every day. And so do Joseph and Giza. I even received a phone call from Evelyn to congratulate me on my decision.

Since my move, I've been struggling to get up in the morning, going through the motions of showering, dressing, swallowing the thoughtful breakfast—cereal with milk on weekends and toast and jelly on weekdays—served to me by my caring hosts.

I shouldn't complain. I have even made a friend of the fruit-store owner on Intervale Avenue. I was buying apples and oranges when he asked, *"Wus noch?"* ("What else?" in Yiddish), smiling broadly after I had put in my order.

I almost choked. It can't be! This man is talking to me in Yiddish! My mother would *love* this!

Do I *look* that Jewish, or do I *sound* Jewish? I debated privately.

"That will be all. Thank you!" I smiled back.

"I was just wondering, are you from Israel?" the man inquired. "I thought I detected an Israeli accent."

"No, I'm from France," I explained.

Only in America! I thought to myself, using Stanley's favorite expression. Only in America would someone feel free enough to ask such a loaded question of a perfect stranger.

I vowed to buy all my fruit and vegetables from him from then on.

What keeps me from really enjoying my new situation is Adele. She didn't say good-bye. She simply gave me a quick, disapproving glance and spoke only four words—"I think you're wrong!"—as Stanley took my suitcase out the door. When I tried to kiss her good-bye, she pulled back, stiff in her tailored suit and impeccable hairdo.

So I sent a long letter to the Millers—for Adele's sake, of course—explaining as best I could that my moving out was actually a tribute to them. They had given me enough confidence to take that big step.

It's good-byes, I now realize, that trouble me, more than changes.

All this preys on my mind and prevents me from fully enjoying the Schenkers' efforts to make me feel at home. It's not easy changing gears, being fussed over and pampered instead of the other way around.

Maman's steady coolness adds, of course, to the shadow that hangs over me. She writes her usually newsy letters—about the latest dinner given by the Chavignats; meeting a radiant, recently engaged Jeanette Blaustein on the street or telling the latest doings of our silly concierge. She totally ignores my job, which I mention in every single letter. She must still be angry at me. But she does add that Fernand was invited for lunch this past Sunday and that he took a walk afterward with Lily and Denise. Not a word about my coming home, however, or who's going to meet me in le Havre. Yet they must have discussed it!

Sometimes—only for a moment—I worry that Fernand may fall in love with Denise or Lily. They're much more attractive than I am, and I'm so far away! But, as long as I get my daily letter—and so far, it has averaged out to that—he must still love me!

Thursday, December 27

Work is the brightest spot in my life these days. Once I get there, everything takes a backseat. It's been six weeks now since I started.

Maria and I continue to get together for the morning coffee breaks. I have also discovered Doreen. I had noticed her in the ladies' room. She has curly red hair, and a peach-colored face full of freckles, and is quite pretty. Maria said that, with her looks and a name like Doreen, she has to be Irish. She is a relative newcomer to the office, and Maria doesn't know much about her. At any rate, Doreen always smiled at me from a distance. And I always smiled back.

Then one day I needed a new ribbon for my typewriter and got stuck trying to remove the used one. Doreen walked over to my desk and offered her services.

"You look as if you could use some help. It's a cinch once you get the knack!" In two minutes she had done the job, with the cool confidence that only one other person I know shares for things mechanical: my sister Lily.

So today, Maria, Doreen, and I have planned to meet during the coffee break to get better acquainted.

Maria was right: Doreen is Irish—but only half, on her mother's side. Her father is German, she explains. Both were born in this country.

"What's the difference?" I want to know. "Your parents are American, since they were born here! Does it matter where their parents came from?"

"Look," says Maria, "people who immigrate here leave their families and roots behind. In this country, you have to learn a new language, a new way of life, meet all sorts of people. Finding a group to belong to is crucial! So people tend to stay with people whose background is the same."

"So you are from France?" Doreen asks me.

"Yes, I'm only here temporarily. I expect to go home in a few months."

"Are you French on both sides?" Doreen asks.

I take a deep breath and decide to tell them exactly what I am. "As a matter of fact, neither of my parents was born in France. My mother came from Hungary and my father from Poland. They both settled in France—my mother in her late teens, my father in his twenties. They're both Jewish."

I hope neither Doreen nor Maria noticed the lowering of my voice as I said *Jewish*. And I realize now that I said "they" are Jewish—meaning my parents—instead of "we" are Jewish.

"Jewish? Really!" Doreen exclaims. "It never occurred to me that you were Jewish. To me, you were French. Period."

"But I *am* French, too. My sisters and I were born there, and my parents became French citizens years ago."

I am surprisingly calm and collected. This is good practice for me!

"It didn't occur to me, either," Maria says. "I guess people don't think there are Jews in France, probably because it's primarily a Catholic country—just like Brazil or other South American countries, for that matter. By the way," she adds, "my husband is Jewish, too."

"You're eating ham in your sandwich," Doreen says to me, puzzled.

"Well, not *all* Jews are observant Jews, you know," I point out. "Most people I know—in France anyway—are not."

We laugh then about how the three of us are just like everyone else, casting people into stereotypes—whether we talk about the Irish, the French, or the Jews.

I feel good—free to be myself, at least with Maria and Doreen. All I need is a lot more practice.

Thursday, January 3

We are in 1952! The gloomy feeling I had has finally lifted. For one thing, Mr. McGibbons complimented me for pointing out a problem. No big deal, really. I simply noticed that subscribers were filed separately under *Anvers, Antwerp,* and *Antwerpen,* when actually the three are the French, English, and Flemish names for the same place.

"It takes a European to know about those things," my boss said. He even had Mr. Cudlip, one of the vice presidents, come and thank me in person for the valuable service I had rendered the company!

For another thing, I've made a new friend: Bill, the editor with the initialed shirt. I prefer to call him William, his given name. He's delighted to be able to talk to someone about France. He was part of the World War II D day landing force—a hero.

Now William and I chat every morning in the coffee line. He is quite charming, and, I must confess, it feels wonderful to have a young man fuss over me. He has always insisted on treating me to coffee or a pastry, and I have always declined. First of all, I certainly don't need the extra food. And then, I can't seem to shake the habit instilled in my sisters and me early on by Maman.

"You don't need anyone to pay your way!" she would always remind us. Even during the war, when everybody was hungry, we were to tell anyone who invited us for a meal that we had already eaten, thank you.

Finally, this morning, William, every bit as stubborn as I am, snapped, "Why can't you let a guy treat you? It's only a cup of coffee!"

It hadn't occurred to me that I was actually depriving him of the pleasure of treating me.

And so I accept!

Thursday, January 24

Adele called yesterday. She got my letter, and I guess she's been thinking about what it said. Not a word or a simple question about how I was doing, though. Her voice all velvety, she tried to wrap me into her life again: elaborating on the last visit to the Rudmans' and Murray's last letter.

She eventually got to the point. "Could you do me a special favor and spend the coming weekend with Rita? I'll be out of town on Saturday and Sunday nights. Of course, Stanley will be here, but it isn't the same! You know how much Rita likes your company!"

At least Adele knows she needs me and no longer takes me for granted, I thought to myself.

"Of course," I agreed. "I'll just go to work straight from Tompkins Square on Monday morning."

"Thanks. No need to tell you how much I appreciate it!"

Appreciate it? Adele is probably the person least likely to know or care how uncomfortable it is for me to return to Tompkins Square.

I don't particularly want to give up my weekend. Sundays have become very precious to me. I alternate them between Giza and the Schenkers, who have truly adopted me. Wherever they go, I go. And so, every other

Sunday, I am invited with them to visit Mrs. Schenker's younger brother, Jack, who lives with his family in a house in the Bronx, a bus ride away from Intervale Avenue.

The truth of the matter is that I think I am developing a crush on Jack—a married man! How is this possible when I *know* I'm as much in love with Fernand as ever! Don't I still dash for the mailbox, write to him almost daily, and count the days until I see him again?

Jack is rather short, slight of build, and has a receding hairline. He could probably be my father! But he has a sensitive face: green eyes under dark eyebrows, tiny lines that radiate around his eyes when he laughs, and a warm smile. What I like best about him, though, is the calm, confident way in which he handles everything. He takes over the kitchen without a fuss at the first sign of panic by his wife, Mancsi, whose name is the same as my mother's. He shows inexhaustible patience with his seven-year-old daughter, Nancy, no matter how often she tugs at his sleeve for attention. And I love to watch him wrap his arms around baby Susie or lift her into the air while the two of them coo blissfully, ignoring Mancsi's pleas of "Careful, Jack! She's just a baby!"

I haven't realized until now how hungry I have been for closeness and touch—how much I have missed my sisters' hugs and affection and Fernand's tenderness.

How I loved walking down the boulevard Saint-Michel with Fernand. How I loved to hold hands with him or to steal light kisses, or later, in the darkness of the last row at the movies, nestle in that tender spot between neck and shoulder. Parting was always hardest for me, so it was understood that I would be the one to hang up first whenever we talked on the telephone at work and that I would be the one to turn the corner first after we parted for the evening.

Sometimes, I sensed how much I expected from him, and it frightened me. Many times I needed to be reassured—God only knows how often—and was dying to ask him, "Do you love me?" But asking would have made me feel like a beggar, and I kept it to myself.

Saturday, January 26

My weekend isn't a waste after all. There is Rita to walk arm in arm with and to cuddle up with while watching TV or reading to her from *Le Petit Prince.*

And there is Stanley to say in his own affectionate way, when I serve them dinner, "Hey, this is delicious! What is it?"

Friday, February 8

Life with the Schenkers is settling into a comforting routine. I always leave the house first and return last. There's no quarrel or disagreement as to who does what in the household. I am being spoiled for the first time in my life, and I like it.

The Schenkers are also helping me with my budget. Every week, after I have paid my room and board, I put some money into a savings account. Once in a while, I allow myself to buy a piece of clothing—a skirt, a blouse—to build a basic wardrobe for work.

One day at the office, Marla, the secretary, asked me, "Didn't you go home last night?"

I realized she had asked because I had worn the same skirt and blouse two days in a row. I'm sure Marla didn't mean to offend me, but I've been conscious ever since about varying my work clothes.

I've had my eyes set on the bright-red coat I saw in a shop window on Clinton Street. If I got it, I could retire my old bottle-green coat, which I never liked in the first place. Maman insisted on a dark color that wouldn't show the spots, but it is a sad color that doesn't help my dark complexion. I want bright colors! I want to be noticed!

There are so many things I'd like to buy. And yet, I can't seem to be able to make a decision when I'm in the store about the few items I *can* afford. Yes. No. Go ahead! You're allowed! I torture myself, walking away a hundred times as if a single purchase were a matter of life and death.

It must be wonderful to be able to choose and buy without giving a second thought to cost! Times have been hard for us ever since we fled from Alsace and left all our comfort behind.

"Things could be worse!" Maman would always remind us. After all, we *did* treat ourselves to croissants on Sundays and holidays, even if it was the plain sort rather than the more expensive butter ones. And so what if we would always buy the Strasbourg sausages instead of the fancier frankfurters? They tasted wonderful to me. It *did* bother me a little, however, not to be able to afford an ice-cream bar, like the other moviegoers during the intermission. "The main thing," Maman liked to point out, "is that we can afford the movie every week!"

And so, we pretended to be grateful for whatever we had.

Still, as I go up and down the brimming rows of clothing, I dream of being able, some day, to buy whatever strikes my fancy.

I'm also trying to decide what gifts to bring back for my mother and sisters. Perhaps lingerie—slips or nightgowns. They're much more reasonably priced here than in Paris. I don't worry about Fernand. I'll bring him back some records. As for Pépée, I'm all set: I've already chosen a baby doll, in pink and blue.

Friday, February 15

Maman would definitely approve of the Schenkers: They look at the good side of everything and they always count their blessings. They're especially grateful to be living in America.

At dinner, they often talk about their only son, Jacques, who was born and educated in France. The Schenkers emigrated without him shortly after the war, thanks to Jack, who sponsored them. When Jacques' own son was born, he decided to join his parents, hoping that America would provide a more secure future for his child. But he didn't like New York and so he moved to Hollywood, where he is quickly becoming a fashionable tailor.

"Believe me, America is still the best land for us Jews," Mrs. Schenker always says. "At least here we have the same opportunities as anyone else, and we can walk with our heads held high!"

I certainly would be the first one to acknowledge that! But does that mean that you *can* dismiss your own country so quickly?

I don't know much about the Schenkers' past. They only bring up fragments of their lives here and there. I know they are both from Hungary and spent the war years in France, hiding in the Free Zone somewhere near Périgueux. But it is obvious that they don't like to talk about it.

I understand them, yet I wonder, how can you possibly leave the country where you were born, where you learned your first words, your first songs, where you shared your first kiss, the place where you first experienced friendship and love and saw the ocean for the first time—so many firsts that helped shape your life?

Can't the Schenkers understand? Can't anyone understand that it is in France, my homeland, that I want to be able to walk with my head high? Is that so wrong?

Sunday, February 17

I love Jack's house, the first real house I've ever been in. Today, when no one is looking, I touch the red brick outside. My eyes linger on the fir tree on the front lawn. As I walk from room to room, from the kitchen to the backyard, I realize what a cramped life I've led, living in tight and uncomfortable quarters in Paris and in a dormitory when in hiding. I want to stretch. And it dawns on me how, after being torn away from family and friends, repeatedly losing beloved homes—in Mulhouse,

Paris, Normandy—I have always dreamed of what may seem trivial to others: a house, like this one. I want loads of nooks and crannies for privacy, windows from which I can gaze at the sky, a yard where I can sink my bare feet into the freshly cut grass, and most of all, a safe place that I can call my own.

No wonder I don't ever want to leave Jack's house when it's time to go!

All this brings me back to the memorable day when I saw the ocean for the first time. One of the young ladies I worked with in Paris, Madeleine, had invited me for a few days to her hometown in Mortain, Normandy. She took me for the day to the coastal town of Jullouville-Bouillon. . . .

It is a hazy day. We are walking over the dunes, toward the water. First I see nothing. And then my eyes detect the line between sea and sky that extends to infinity, and I wonder—as I still do now, even though I know the scientific facts—how all that water doesn't spill into the atmosphere.

Breathing in the salty air in greedy gulps, I run barefoot on the shore to the edge of the water, where the breaking waves lap at my ankles with their tiny, icy, biting tongues. I wave at the sea gulls circling over me, howling as loudly as they do.

I settle down into a sloping dune, my chin on my knees, immobile, afraid to disturb the lives of the tiny beings, visible and invisible, in the sand. And I watch in endless fascination each wave as it rushes to the shore, crashing noisily on the sand in a fringe of silver foam, only to come to life again in the shape of another wave, stronger and louder than before.

I no longer feel alone, but rooted in the dune, much like the barnacles clinging to the rocks in the nearby cove. I take in the sunlight, the water, the sand, the birds clamoring above my head. I feel as I've never felt before—serene and, at long last, at one with the universe.

I have found my niche, and I refuse to be dislodged when it's time to leave.

Thursday, February 21

Doreen has been looking upset these days. She doesn't smile and has kept to herself. Something must be the matter.

"Is anything wrong?" I finally ask this morning, catching her in the hallway.

"I'll tell you later, during coffee break," she whispers.

There *is* something wrong.

Doreen, on the verge of tears, later confides to Maria and me that the young man, George, whom she's been dating for several weeks now has not called her this week, which means she won't be going out with him this coming Saturday.

Saturdays are special, Doreen explains. If a man hasn't called you by Tuesday, there's little chance that he'll take you out on Saturday. Meaning, as everyone here knows it, that he is probably going out with someone else.

"He told me he'd call me!" Doreen laments. "But he never did. It's already Thursday!"

Why would anyone promise to call and not keep his promise? What kind of games do people play here? I wonder. And why would a girl want to go out with someone just for the sake of being out on Saturday night?

"Don't get yourself so worked up!" Maria advises. "I know there's a lot of pressure on girls to be popular—and being out on a date on Saturday means that you are popular," she explains for my benefit. "Look," she continues, putting her arm around Doreen, "I got very upset the first couple of times it happened to me. I'd meet this very nice, charming fellow. He'd take my phone number and promise to call me. And I'd believe him! When he didn't call, I'd be simply devastated!

"Listen to me: If a guy isn't being truthful, what do you need him for? You're better off reading a good book! And if you feel blue, you're welcome to come to my house for dinner. And that goes for you, too!" she adds, turning to me.

"Thanks!" Doreen smiles. "At least I know you mean it!"

I decline Maria's invitation. This weekend I have plans to see Joseph. "Thanks!" I say, appreciating her understanding. "Maybe another time!"

The whole scene makes me glad I don't have to worry about dating here!

Friday, February 29

Mrs. Mayer and I are sitting comfortably on the living-room sofa while Mr. Mayer and the Schenkers are playing cards. It feels especially cozy this evening because it's snowing lightly outside. The Mayers are best friends of the Schenkers and often visit to play cards.

Mrs. Mayer is raving about Budapest—an exquisite city divided by the Danube into Buda and Pest—as if she left it yesterday. As I listen to her, I think of my mother, who was born and raised in Budapest, too. How I wish now that I knew more about that time of her life! She must have been homesick when she moved to Strasbourg, no matter how beautiful her new hometown was. She has never gone back.

"I give you a lot of credit for coming to New York alone—even though you lived with a family," Mrs. Mayer continues. "That didn't turn out too well, did it? It's too bad. I'm saying this because I wasn't happy at all when I first arrived here. And I came here with my mother and father! I just didn't feel at home. It took me every bit of two years not to *like* it, mind you, but just to get *used* to it! Of course, I wouldn't live anywhere else today!

"It's strange," she ponders, pausing for a moment to look at me. "I went back home six years later. The street was just the way I left it, with the same stores, the same buildings. I even recognized a couple of passersby in the neighborhood. The odd thing was that *I* had changed. I had gotten used to taller buildings, a wider variety of people. I was concerned with different issues.

"People at home look at you differently when you go back," she goes on. "For them, you've become 'American'—whatever that means. I think they sense the change in you, your having seen another part of the world, your having a broader view. In a strange way, they feel let down, rejected because you left. So, here you are, a foreigner in America and an American in Europe!"

As I listen, I am wondering if, on my return to Paris, I will find the rooms of our apartment smaller, our street more narrow, the shops less spacious than in my memory, just as I did on my return from the convent after the war.

VI

SPRING

SPRING 1952

Monday, March 17

The return home is beginning to feel real to me: I have
booked my passage aboard the *Ile-de-France* for the middle of May. I'll be sharing a cabin with three lady passengers, just as on the *Liberté*.

Whenever I think about it, I feel a slight twinge in my
stomach. There are so many things I still need to do
before I go. Will there be enough time? Will I have
enough money? Will I even feel sure I am doing the right
thing?

Adele hasn't even had the decency to call me since I
spent the weekend on Tompkins Square. As for my

mother, I seem to have a hard time calling her Maman these days—will she ever talk to me again? I mean *really* talk? She hasn't yet referred to my return. The closest she came to it was when she confirmed that Fernand was definitely going to be drafted into the army at the beginning of July. She must still feel outraged at my decision.

So what's going to happen? I have visions of her not waiting for me at St. Lazare station, of giving me the silent treatment when I get home. It's when I'm alone that I feel worst. Sometimes I can't fall asleep, and when I do, I dream of smoldering trees and I wake up oppressed, panting, unable to catch my breath, just as I did in the convent when I missed home.

The office is still my best refuge. There, at least, I don't have much time to think, and many good things have been happening to me. I'm perfectly able to answer the telephone now; it no longer frightens me. Furthermore, I don't have to refer to the French word or expression as often to get the real meaning of an English word. In fact, I've learned some professional terms specific to printing and trade magazines that I don't even know in French!

And then, the other morning, Gwen and Tina came in with the exact same dress on: black-and-white polka-dot with a white collar. They looked at one another in disbelief, and then Gwen began to laugh so hard that the rest of us joined in. A good story to write home about!

Most of the time I try to appreciate what every day brings and enjoy it to the fullest. Who would have thought, for instance, that I would get not one but *four* invitations for the seder next week? Bernard and Esther Singer invited me, which was very nice. I haven't seen them since my first and only visit, but they have telephoned me once in a while. And then Maria, in the office, asked me, too.

"Are you invited somewhere for the seder?" she said. "If not, you're welcome to my house! Even though I was not born a Jew, I can turn out an outstanding traditional meal—at least, that's what my husband says!"

"Thanks! I'd love to accept if I hadn't promised someone else already," I said.

The Schenker family invited me, too. But I long ago promised to go to Giza's for the occasion. As she put it, "I'm sorry we don't keep all the Jewish holidays. But we have always observed Passover and, of course, Rosh Hashanah and Yom Kippur." She even invited the Millers, though she knew Adele would decline.

Celebrating holidays is certainly central to American life. Everyone gets into the act: the radio, the TV, the card shops, the stores. It must be just as unthinkable for a Jew *not* to have a seder to go to for Passover as it is for a gentile *not* to be invited for Christmas. This does give one a sense of belonging, but it also forces one into a group.

What stands out for me in all this is that in this country—at least in New York—all the holidays are treated equally. The radio and the TV remind all the listeners about *all* the holidays, religious and otherwise, and let them know whether the parking regulations are in effect or not. The message is loud and clear: It is all right to be what you are—Catholic, Protestant, Jewish, or anything else.

I wish it were that open in France. I bet that the average French person has never even heard of the word *seder!*

Passover. I am looking forward to the seder. I only

remember fragments of celebrations from before the war: lavish and elaborate preparations by my mother of the traditional dishes—I remember in particular the two gefilte fish, one sweet, one salty—and the special set of Limoges china only used for the occasion. My father read from a text in Hebrew and later explained that the special crystal glass of wine set aside was for Elijah, a mysterious and invisible visitor—a prophet—who was to appear later. All evening, I kept my eyes on the door and watched the level of wine in the glass. No one turned up, and the glass remained full.

My mother is quite interested in my detailed account of the many invitations I received for Passover, particularly the one from Bernard.

And yes, she has received my money order, which always comes in very handy. I've been able to send her forty dollars every month since I started to work. Maman writes about everything except my return!

In a separate letter, Denise says that she herself is very excited about my coming home soon. Do I intend to return to the same job or am I going to look for another job where I could use my English? she wants to know. She has begun to skim through the newspaper ads, just for the fun of it.

Well, I certainly am not thinking *that* far ahead at the moment.

What interests me more is her mentioning that "we" will be waiting at St. Lazare station. I wonder if that includes my mother? I can't bring myself to ask.

At least Fernand is getting ready for the big event. He wants to know what my cabin number is, he writes, so that he can greet me the very minute the ship docks!

Both Fernand and Denise want to know how the seder was at Giza's. And so I am writing a detailed account to Fernand tonight and asking him to tell my sister all about it.

There were seven of us. Joseph asked his friend Mark, from school, and his parents. The apartment looked very different. Giza had put away much of the clutter. The table was elegantly set, with a festive tablecloth and crystal glasses.

Giza immediately got me involved. "The ladies of the house are supposed to light the candles. Let's get that out of the way."

I nodded eagerly. It was a privilege.

She suggested I sit across from Joseph and his father, who both led the seder. I noted that the four men wore yarmulkes. I felt as if I were in the first row in a special class where I finally learned something I always sensed but never exactly knew.

I didn't miss a thing, from the seven symbolic ingredients on the small plate, the prayer that accompanied every gesture and the breaking of the matzoh, to the drinking of the sweet wine. When Joseph began to read from the Haggadah in English, articulating every sentence, I knew it was for my benefit. The others read, too, in a way that helped me understand everything.

I listened with a new feeling of pride about the Jews' courage in fleeing from Egypt to escape slavery, their ingenuity in facing and outwitting the enemy, their unflinching faith and resilience. I sensed that we were commemorating a part of our history, a tradition that had been carried on for centuries before us. What did it matter that I didn't believe in the God that Joseph was reading about, or in elusive Elijah, and that the prayers and the songs were unfamiliar. It was something I was a part of, our heritage, whether I believed or not.

Too bad I don't know anyone in Paris who observes Passover. Where am I going to go to seder next year?

Saturday, April 12

I woke up early this Saturday ready to do as much as I could. There are only four Saturdays left. Of course, the idea of seeing Paris and everybody again is terribly exciting. Yet, the idea of leaving is beginning to make me anxious; who knows if I'll ever come back? There's something so final about leaving.

There are no two ways about it: I've got to go to the Apollo today. How can I face Fernand and not have seen that fabled Harlem theater from the outside, if not from inside?

I decide to walk all the way. "Are you crazy?" they all said when I first told what I planned to do.

The sun is out, the air is brisk. I put on my most comfortable shoes and my old green coat. Mr. Schenker insists on giving me an apple and a ham-and-cheese sandwich on fresh rye bread rich in caraway seeds.

I look at my watch: It is exactly eleven-fifteen. I am at the corner of 163rd Street and Intervale Avenue.

Walking down Intervale Avenue is monotonous and bleak with the elevated train blocking the sky. The stores are uninteresting. The walk improves when I near the bridge over the Harlem River that links the Bronx to Manhattan. The bridge is firm under my feet. I am the only one walking across the pedestrian path. The car drivers whipping by me must think I'm crazy, but I happen to like bridges. Especially in New York City, where everything is so spread out and the different boroughs are each a world unto themselves. Bridges give you a solid sense of connection.

I am in Harlem. As I look around, I find myself to be the only white person, an odd and uncomfortable feeling for me. I am once again a minority.

There is more street life, here, though. People are gathered at street corners, lost in animated discussions. Others are bunched up around a young man speaking nonstop as he does card tricks on a corrugated box. People walk leisurely, taking the time to greet one another or call out to one another across the street. There are plenty of children playing on the side streets. Sports clothes and sneakers are the weekend uniform here just as they are elsewhere in the city, but here they are more colorful, and here and there you come across a young man or woman dressed in a very flamboyant outfit.

The avenues with their cluttered stores, the side streets with their bleak brownstones or their look-alike redbrick apartment complexes separated from one another by patches of green are so similar that I often lose track of where I am.

At last, 125th Street! The street of Fernand's Apollo! It's more to the west, and so I walk in that direction. The building is hardly distinguishable from the others around it. No towers. No dome. A plain entrance with ordinary lettering for that world-famous concert hall!

Disappointed for both of us, I head back east and continue my walk downtown, looking for a Horn and Hardart or a Chock Full o'Nuts—a familiar spot where I can rest, enjoy a cup of coffee, and feel at home in a strange neighborhood. There are none in sight. I will have to wait until 86th Street, where, according to Mrs. Mayer, there is one—if I can last that long!

Why aren't there any benches for people to sit on, I wonder. Then I realize the sidewalks are too narrow for benches or sidewalk cafés. The message is loud and clear: No time for dawdling here. New Yorkers are not dawdlers. They don't, like the Parisians, watch the Seine for hours from the bridges, or meander through the streets on market days, or browse by the *bouquinistes* (second-hand-book stalls) along the Seine, or spend the better part of a weekend afternoon sitting at the terrace of a café talking to a friend and watching the people go by.

New York City is a place always in motion, where old buildings disappear to make room for new ones, where you can do the things you wouldn't dare do at home—or never could—and be the person you always wanted to be but could not. It is a place where you can belong and yet be an individual.

I cut across Fifth Avenue and suddenly I'm in another world. Exhausted, I let myself fall onto a bench along Central Park, facing the New York of the movies: canopied, modern apartment buildings, doormen helping elegant people step out of cabs or private cars.

The sandwich Mr. Schenker gave me tastes wonderful, as does the apple. They restore some of my strength. Off I go again down the avenue. It's past two o'clock when I reach Eighty-sixth Street.

Eighty-sixth Street is a surprise for me, having many shops with German wares. I recognize the familiar *gen-*

darmes sausages hanging from the butchers' ceilings, the same wonderful variety of cold cuts and delicacies as are displayed in any French *charcuterie*. There is a *konditorei*—a tea room—and a kind of shop I've never seen before, one that specializes in marzipan, shaped like fruit and animals. The street is wide and full of eager shoppers. Two women pass by me, conversing in German. I get a heartwarming sense of being in Europe.

There is my Horn and Hardart. I spot an empty table, where I drop my coat—since it's Saturday the cafeteria is crowded with shoppers and children—and I dash to the coffee-dispensing machine. I take an empty cup, place it on the receptacle, and out comes the milk and the coffee from the magic faucets.

I am tempted by the freshly baked pies and cakes displayed in the nearby showcase. I opt for the cheesecake, my favorite New York cake, one that doesn't exist in Paris. I insert the required dime and nickel in the slot and pull the display case open. I savor both my coffee and cake, keenly aware that this may be my last New York treat.

I continue my route down Lexington Avenue, then move back to Madison Avenue. Here, there are small, elegant boutiques that remind me of Faubourg-St. Honoré in Paris. The quiet side streets with their glances of Central Park one block away are lovely. People here are dressed in the latest fashion, their hair cut in the latest style. They carry shopping bags from the fancy stores: Henri Bendel, Saks Fifth Avenue, Bergdorf Goodman.

I move over to Fifth Avenue at Fifty-seventh Street. There is always a hustle and bustle at this particular spot —people crossing hurriedly before the light changes and the traffic takes over. I glance at Tiffany's windows.

I move on down Fifth Avenue. I must see Saks Fifth Avenue and St. Patrick's Cathedral. From a distance, St. Patrick's appears squeezed between two department stores. It is, however, on a block by itself. The sharp, elegant, Gothic lines and the majestic, soaring spire remind me of French churches and contrast sharply with the massive, square constructions nearby.

I climb the steps to the front entrance. Inside, the church looks, feels, and smells familiar. I spot the statue of the Virgin Mary, the stations of the cross. But it is the statue of St. Joseph I am looking for. I've had a soft spot in my heart for him since my days in the convent. No one ever made a fuss over him, I thought, and yet, he was good to Mary and brought up Jesus as if he were his own flesh and blood. It couldn't have been easy raising a boy with ideas so different from other boys.

The pause is restful. But it makes me realize how exhausted I am. Should I stop here or go on? I ask myself.

This is my last chance to see New York. I will go on.

Saks Fifth Avenue looks quite crowded, and I am too tired to waste my steps in a store. I am much more taken by the promenade at Rockefeller Center. At least there are benches for strollers! I sit and remember coming here with Rita and Stanley, when they went ice-skating. It seems like years ago.

The last stretch is the longest. My knees are giving out, but I am determined to go as far as Fourteenth Street and Irving Place for a last cup of coffee at Horn and Hardart. I used to stop there when I went to Klein's from the Millers'.

Five more, three more blocks! I tell myself along the way. I can't give up so close to the goal! I finally get there. Bronx to Union Square, Manhattan. Five and a half hours! I feel as proud as if I had achieved a world record.

No time for a movie today. Only time to head back home by subway for dinner, "The Hit Parade," and "Your Show of Shows" with Sid Caesar.

=====

Tonight, Sid Caesar does a Japanese spoof. The incredible thing is that in the middle of his gibberish, which definitely sounds Japanese to my foreign ears, he manages to blend in Yiddish words. I laugh and I cry as always; and, as always, I remember more of the Yiddish words my grandmother spoke.

I wonder what Sid Caesar's life was like when he was growing up?

Wouldn't it be wonderful if every sad or troubled person could turn into a comedian?

Me included.

Sunday, April 20

We are going to New Brunswick, New Jersey—my first trip out of New York and out of state.

"We can't let Renée go back to Paris without visiting the Barths!" Mrs. Schenker declared. So off we all go in Jack's station wagon; Jack's family, the Schenkers, and me.

We are soon going over a bridge, the George Washington Bridge, much wider and more open than any I've seen so far. The cables that hold it soar in majestic and bold lines against the sky. The large river below is shimmering in the sun.

"The Hudson River!" Jack announces proudly.

"How beautiful!" I exclaim.

WELCOME TO NEW JERSEY! a sign reads.

We are entering a maze of highways, each with large signs pointing to many directions. God help the out-of-town tourist who doesn't know the area and must make a quick decision! But Jack drives along comfortably and doesn't seem to mind the many cars passing him by.

I lose interest when we enter an industrial zone, a myriad of factories and refineries. We close the windows to keep out the stench that is filling the air.

I am relieved when we finally find ourselves in areas where whole towns are made of white wood-frame homes and manicured lawns along pleasant tree-lined streets with, in places, special paths for bicycles. How different from the area in the Bronx where Jack lives, where only a few private homes are mixed in with the many apartment buildings.

We have arrived. Exclamations pour out of the doorway of the redbrick, two-story house where Jack has stopped: "Renée! Bertha! Willie!"

How heartwarming to see the white-haired, tired-faced Mrs. Barth I remember smile a genuine, carefree smile, and the wiry, always-worried Mr. Barth of my youth rush to me and hug me. The people who welcomed me to Paris twelve years ago are welcoming me in America!

It's only now that I see Eva. She was about fifteen when I last saw her, and she is now in her middle twenties. She is beaming, genuinely happy to have us all around her.

"Who would have thought that we would meet again in the United States!" she exclaims. "Let me take a good look at you!"

Two blond children, of about six and four, appear in the doorway, somewhat puzzled by the gathering on the front lawn.

"Come on, Mark, Isabelle. Come and meet Renée, a friend from Paris. And say hello to Aunt Bertha and Uncle Willie and everybody!"

They take a few shy steps and stretch out limp hands to meet mine.

Eva's husband, a burly, friendly man, rushes down the steps.

"Honey," Eva says, "this is Renée, the eldest Roth daughter. You remember, I told you about how the whole family stayed with us when they first arrived in Paris?"

She has hardly any accent, at least to my ears. How fascinating! The French accent is so difficult to overcome.

"Sure!" he replies, shaking my hand vigorously. "Welcome to New Brunswick!"

He moves to greet the others, and I hear him address the Barths as Mom and Dad. They, in turn, seem genuinely fond of him.

Mrs. Barth walks over to me, embracing me warmly all over again.

"It's so wonderful to see you! I wish your mother were here, too!"

"I take it you don't miss France?" I ask.

"France, no. The few friends I left there, yes. But I have new friends here. Imagine, right here in New Brunswick, they have an association for Jews from Hungary!"

No one mentions Violette, lying in the cemetery in Bagneux, near Paris, but she is on our minds. She is partly the reason they are all here, so that the tragic circumstances that took her away won't happen to them again.

"We'll be having lunch in about fifteen minutes!" Eva announces. "Does anyone want a cold drink?"

"Yes, I do!" Jack and Nancy say.

"Come on in, then," Eva urges, leading the way.

"You're coming in, too, Renée?" Mrs. Barth inquires.

"In a little while!" I reply.

I need a few moments to myself to adjust the image of the Barths as I knew them in Paris to the Barths as they are now, content and, at least on the surface, well adjusted to their new land.

Eva rushes down the steps.

"How do you find my mother and father?" she asks. "Don't they look great? They wanted to be on their own, but Burt convinced them to live with us. They have their own apartment on the second floor. My husband is a real sweetheart. And I have two lovely children. I'm so very lucky!" she adds.

She wants to know about my mother, my sisters, my life in Paris. I tell her about Fernand, too, and about how I miss Paris.

She doesn't, she says—just maybe once in a while when she has a chance to speak French. Actually, she doesn't seek out French people. Most of her friends are Americans. She and her husband belong to the local Jewish temple, and most of their friends do, too. "I'm quite happy here!" she concludes.

"How do you do it—I mean, speaking without an accent?" I ask.

"It happened quite naturally. At the beginning, I made a conscious effort, and when my children were born, I took a couple of classes. I didn't want them to make fun of me.

"Come now, let's join the others. . . . You must be hungry!"

Maybe, I reflect as I follow her inside, her eagerness to forget about the past—Paris, the hideous war, her sister's death—has helped quicken her adjustment to this new, welcoming land. How wonderful that she could start a fresh life without ever looking back. I envy her. Yet, I wonder how anyone can cut out such a vital part of themselves.

The trick is to go on.

Thursday, April 24

It is definite: Fernand is taking the first train to le Havre out of St. Lazare station—the mere mention of the station thrills me—so that he will be at the dock in plenty of time to meet me. I can't believe that the separation—sixteen months, five days—is coming to an end, and that I will soon be able to touch Fernand, to kiss his smile, to hear his voice.

I look at myself in the mirror. I carry my head higher these days. I am certainly less shy, and I'm full of so many questions. I hope he'll recognize me. The eyes, the smile are still the same. I wonder if he'll like my haircut with bangs in the front?

How will it feel, kissing him after all these months of waiting?

I don't want to think about my mother yet. She won't be waiting for me in le Havre; that much I'm sure of! We'll have plenty of time to decide what to do about her. Fernand has rescued me many times before.

The crying spells have started again, taking me by surprise.

They started this past Saturday—at the movies, where I usually end my afternoon. I had done well in my last-minute errands—buying two Dixieland jazz recordings for Fernand. The film was about marines on a ship. Something stirred in me as the crew began to sing "The Star-Spangled Banner." Tears burned my eyes, rolling down my cheeks.

I had to stop and think: What are the tears about? It is change, I decided. Good things have happened to me in America, and it's difficult to leave. And so I cried on. I cried, too, for my mother, who hasn't even told me she welcomes me back. And I cried for France, the country I love but that hasn't loved me enough.

The movie over, I ran for the closest Horn and Hardart, waiting for the mood to pass. There, at least, I could stay forever. There are no garçons, like those in the Paris cafés who hover around you and keep asking if you want another *café crème* or *citron pressé*.

I have had to force myself out of bed in the morning ever since then, even to go to work.

"What's wrong?" William asks. "You've been frowning all week!"

Most of the time, when I feel the tears well up, I duck behind my desk long enough to blink them back.

When I am alone in my room after the Schenkers have retired for the night now, a weakness sneaks up from my toes, inches up my legs, reaches my chest. Within seconds, my heart is racing, my temples are throbbing, my forehead is covered with beads of perspiration.

It will pass, I tell myself. There's no reason to alarm anyone.

I get up to shake the feeling, but it doesn't go away. Instead, the numbness reaches my neck.

"I don't feel well!" I finally called out last night, frightened to death, hearing someone tinkering in the kitchen.

Within seconds, Mrs. Schenker was at my side. "Willie! Quick! Hand me a towel soaked in cold water!" she yelled.

Mr. Schenker rushed to my bed. "What's the matter?" he asked. "Are you sick to your stomach?"

"No, it isn't my stomach. I don't know what it is. I wish I knew what's playing such tricks on me."

The cool water felt good on my forehead.

"Maybe you should go to bed and have a good night's sleep!" Willie suggested.

"No . . . No . . . it's early yet!"

The last thing I wanted was to be left alone.

I tried to sleep with the door open and the night-table light on.

Tonight, I have settled into the sofa. I'm trying to watch the TV, which is showing, of all things, something about the "twilight zone." But I can't concentrate. I am anticipating the first signs of my distress and I am terrified.

There it is, sneaking up on me again. First, the tingling in my toes, changing into numbness, reaching my legs, my thighs, my stomach. It is getting to my chest again. I clutch the side of the sofa to force myself up. My heart begins racing, my temples throb. In seconds, my forehead is dripping with perspiration. This time, I am going to faint and die!

I hear a trickle of a voice—mine—gather enough strength to whisper, "It's starting again!"

"Willie! A wet towel, please!" Mrs. Schenker yells out.

"Maybe we should get a doctor," he suggests, a worried expression on his face.

"No! No!" I scream.

"Let me call Irma first," Mrs. Schenker decides. "She used to be a nurse." Seconds later, she informs us that the Mayers are coming right over.

The mere sight of Mrs. Mayer walking in fifteen minutes later reassures me. By now, my heart is calmer and the numbness less pronounced, though not entirely gone.

"Well, well. You've given us quite a scare, Renée!" she teases.

"I have scared myself even more!" I say, as I feel a crooked, tentative smile form on my face.

Mr. Mayer suggests some hot tea for all of us.

"How do you feel now?" Mrs. Mayer asks, taking off her glasses to examine my face, feeling my pulse.

"I feel better. Calmer, I mean. But I still feel weak, and I have palpitations off and on."

"It looks like a panic attack to me," Mrs. Mayer pronounces.

That means I'm not going to die! I think to myself.

"Tell me," Mrs. Mayer wants to know, "have you ever had this happen to you before?"

"During the war," I tell her. "Sometimes I had trouble catching my breath, and I thought I was going to die, too. It happened in the cemetery once and when I was worried about my parents after Paris was bombed and thought the war would never end. Of course, I was much younger then!"

"Is something bothering you now?" Mrs. Mayer asks.

I feel the weight of things impossible to explain.

"I've been thinking a lot about my leaving. Of course, I'm very happy at the idea of returning home, but," I add, a bit hesitant, "my mother isn't thrilled about my coming home just yet. But Fernand, my boyfriend, is going into the army soon, and I've got to see him before he leaves!"

"It certainly sounds reasonable enough to me. It looks as if you might get sick if you *don't* go home!" she continues.

Now here is someone who understands! She is putting into simple words what I've struggled so long to think through.

"What if my sisters want to come to America? After I've left, Adele won't want to sponsor them! I feel badly about denying them the opportunity!"

Actually, Denise has never mentioned wanting to come. As far as Lily is concerned, it couldn't be further from her mind. What if, I suddenly wonder, it is *my mother* who wants to come to America?

Mrs. Mayer has the most wonderfully reassuring smile. "Is that what's been bothering you?" she says. "From what I know of Mrs. Miller, she hasn't said her last word. If, say, Denise wants to come to the United States, Mrs. Miller may be thrilled to sponsor her, providing she lives with her, the way you did!

"Look, Renée," she says, taking my hand. "I can see that you're concerned about your sisters getting their chance, too. If either of them is really interested, I'll be happy to sponsor them myself. I'm sure the Schenkers would do it, too, but they haven't been here long enough yet."

I stare at the collar of her dress until the lace pattern stops swimming under my gaze. This is America for you! I think to myself. Someone I met only recently is opening her heart and home to me. And she isn't even Jewish!

"Thanks!" I say, hiding my face in her shoulder, hugging her with all my might. "It's very generous of you. I promise you'll never regret it."

"I'll have to discuss it with my husband, of course," Mrs. Mayer goes on. "Come now, let's join the others in the kitchen!"

I won't write home the good news: I'll *tell* them about it. I can't wait to see my mother's face when she learns about the Mayers' offer.

======

The Mayers are very wise. They remind me to apply for a reentry permit. It will allow me to return if I so decide, and give me two years to make up my mind.

Thursday, May 8

Things are much clearer now.

So what if my mother refuses to give me her blessings? I'll just have to learn to live with that unless I want to remain a child the rest of my life. She *has* written to the Schenkers—whom she found for me, I remind myself—to thank them for all they've done for me. All things considered, how can I feel anger toward her?

She performed that first miracle: getting our French naturalization in time. She found the impossible: a military truck to help the family flee from Alsace to the safety of a mountain village on the way to Paris. She found us an apartment in Paris when no one else could. She took serious risks in getting false ID papers for herself and my father. Can I fault her for *forcing* me to come to America any more than I can fault her for sending my sisters and me off to Normandy? She saved our lives, didn't she? Would I rather *not* have come to the United States—where I have learned to know myself in ways I never did before?

"Maman," I'll tell her. "We've got to talk. Some things need to be expressed, not just understood! No more screaming or sticking your fingers in your ears; no more keeping my eyes on you while you turn your back to me; we must talk heart to heart."

I have come up with a long list of things I want to tell her so that she will know the truth about me—even the fact that, when I was four, I *really* did steal the change from our neighbor's milk jug to buy some chocolate-mouse candies, which she has refused to believe all these years.

Maybe she loves me in ways I don't know? And part of that may be wanting me to do all the things she never did, like going to America.

But I have a choice. And my choice is to go back home, because that's what I *need* to do now.

Friday, May 16

The day has come.

Rita, Joseph, and Stanley are seeing me off.

I am sad, and I don't try to fight it. I am sorry to leave the little world of my office—Mr. McGibbons, Doreen, Maria, William, and all the others. They had a little party for me, and Mr. McGibbons gave me a wonderful letter of recommendation.

Joseph and Rita look sad, too. Joseph suddenly appears taller, his face more adult. Rita has also grown, and lost her girlish look. I have grown as well. I left home an ordinary girl, and I am going back enriched by new experiences and a new language that has helped me to express myself in ways I never have before.

"I'm going to miss you two!" I say, putting my arms around them. Rita is wiping her eyes. I wish partings were easier. "I'll write . . . I promise!" I say, feeling a lump grow in my throat.

Stanley puts his arm around her. "She'll be fine," he says.

As for Adele, we've made a peace of a sort. She phoned me to wish me a bon voyage. "I've reread your letter," she said. "Perhaps I've been unfair. . . . Let's part good friends. You're welcome anytime!"

Maybe this time she means it.

At least Stanley is here—as he has always been.

Now I can leave! The two new suitcases, gifts of Giza and the Schenkers, are at my side. They are filled, like my head, with both old and new stuff.

The foghorn blows, calling the passengers aboard.

"Got to go!"

I hug everybody—Joseph, Stanley, Rita last. "Thanks for everything!"

I grab a suitcase with each hand. I pass by a customs officer—the same, I think, who let me in sixteen months ago. He winks at me. Does he recognize me? At any rate, I wink at him, too. I'll be back someday! my smile says.

I want to kiss Rita again, but I am rushing, already on my way home, turning back every other step to rest my suitcases and wave in her direction. The buildings downtown are dazzling in the distance—tall and majestic, soaring against the horizon, the image of the future. No, people don't come to America to dwell on the past, but to make a better life for tomorrow. Somewhere across the vast ocean, I see my mother smiling. I got her what she had wanted all along, her long-cherished wish: an open door to the United States.

I cast a last glance at the sky, no longer framed by a window or obscured by the towering buildings of the city.

"Papa," I say out loud, "I hope you're proud of me and what I've done—even though I am a girl!"

Then I disappear in the gangway.

EPILOGUE

The return to France turned into a disaster: Fernand was indeed eagerly waiting for me at the pier in le Havre. But we were both so overjoyed to be reunited we misread the departure time of the boat train to Paris. That was the last train out to Paris, so we had to spend the night in le Havre. However, my mother remained convinced that it had been planned all along and she did not talk to me for a whole week!

In time, life returned to normal. Fernand joined the military for the expected two years. Fortunately, he was able to arrange to remain in the Paris vicinity. In the meantime, as I settled into a new job working as a bilingual secretary for the Gimbel-Saks Purchasing Office, I couldn't help reflecting, day after day, on the new freedom I had experienced in New York as a Jew. I shared those feelings with Fernand, and we decided to try to make a home in the United States. We got married right after he left the military—and I returned to New York, alone, the day before my reentry permit expired. Fernand joined me six months later.

In the meantime, Mrs. Mayer kept her promise and sponsored Denise, who decided to follow me to the United States. She eventually married and settled in New York.

Lily married someone she had met in the school choir, and they have two sons. She remained in Paris.

Fernand, who became a cutter for men's clothing, liked many things about New York but was still somewhat restless and unhappy about working in the garment industry. He decided to attend Pratt Institute while I continued to work. He did run away one spring morning after six years of marriage, and the traumatic event ended up in a painful divorce.

To keep busy, I decided to return to school and, while supporting myself, completed college and a master's degree in social work at Hunter College—and thus began a new and challenging career. I was remarried in 1968.

My mother did emigrate in the early sixties. Despite her age—she was by then in her late fifties—she adapted rather quickly. (She had begun to learn English while still in Paris.) She took great pride in living independently while working in the garment district. She especially enjoyed being reunited with her Hungarian friends and delighted in the Jewish theater. She also took a special interest in American history.

I really believe that the final chapter of Maman's life

was her happiest. Her last words to me when she died of a heart attack in 1984 were, "Thanks for everything."

How did I come to write?

For one thing, I had made a vow to God during the bombings of D day (I was not quite thirteen): If he let us survive, I'd become a nun. For years, I carried this secret in my soul. I was torn between the Jewish religion, which I hardly knew and had only caused me profound shame and humiliation, and the Catholic faith, which had welcomed my sisters and me with comforting arms.

And then I, who had come to New York to put some distance between myself and my painful past, found it impossible to close that gap. Instead, as I was faced daily with a strong, assertive Jewish culture, I was forced to rethink all my life, to face the unavoidable question: Who am I?

And so, I reconstructed the France of my past in *Touch Wood* and my coming to terms with it in *Safe Harbors*.

The publication of *Touch Wood* in France precipitated a series of wonderful events: One of the people mentioned in the book—now an elderly, blind lady residing in a home for the aged—first heard about it at a formal dinner in town. She in turn alerted the mayor of Flers, in Normandy. Soon, long-lost friends were contacting me through my French publisher. We organized a reunion in the little town of Flers, a "pilgrimage" with the local TV crew to the barn where we had taken refuge after the bombings of D day, all of which culminated in my being awarded the town's Medal of Honor for "making history."

The publication of the book also brought unexpected joy: the reunion, after forty-seven years, in Paris with the last survivor of the nuns who had taken in my sisters and me: seventy-two-year-old Sister Madeleine Malolepszy. She was awarded the Medal of the Righteous Gentiles by Yad Vashem in Jerusalem on June 14, 1993.

Last but not least, it enabled me to meet with countless "hidden children" who confided, "It happened to me, too."

The many letters I received from adults and especially children from both sides of the Atlantic, all acknowledging the need for tolerance and compassion, made me feel that my voice was being heard and that my experience had not been for nought.

In conclusion, I feel very lucky indeed: Not only did I survive the war, but I had the incredible good fortune to be able to come to New York. Rough as it may have felt at the time, I was able to shed, day by day, the deep shame that had been etched in me and to reclaim my Jewish identity as best I could, to learn to laugh again, and to experience a new language that allowed me to express myself in ways I never could before—to have the freedom to become what I am today.

I am thankful for having lived long enough to tell my story to the world and to be able to say thank you not only to those who saved me and my sisters from a certain death but also to those who have reached out to me along the bumpy and arduous road to recovery.

I no longer find it painful to go to France, as it was for many years, when it hurt to connect—and to disconnect. I have made my peace and can now walk the streets of Paris with loving eyes and my head held high. I am no longer hiding or ashamed. I know I can return to Paris, my hometown after Mulhouse, anytime. But I know that my true home is in America.